I0684480

CONTENTS

Naughty Desires

Sexy Stories Collection

VOLUME 43

10 EROTIC SHORT STORIES

TENA SELDAN

Naughty Desires/ Tena Seldan. -- 1st ed.
Xplicit Press, an imprint of TLM Media LLC

ISBN-13: 978-1-62327-574-7
ISBN-10: 1-62327-574-1
eISBN 978-1-62327-624-9

Printed in the United States of America

1 S.H.E. ROBOT: PERFECT LOVER?

Preface

I couldn't believe it. I was finally a star in my own right. If I didn't see my name on the front of the magazine I was looking at or on the dozens of boxes of movies I had made, I wouldn't believe it. I can't believe my eyes; on the front of the "Player" magazine I am holding it says "Ladies Man: Starring Robbie Grinder". This is my 10th feature film and I have finally made it in the porn business.

It may not be a big deal to most people, but it is a major accomplishment for me. I have worked long and hard (no pun intended) to get where I am at in the porn industry and it hasn't been easy. Well, I take that back. I am not complaining about having the opportunity to fuck dozens and dozens of hot and sexy women all year long, that's for sure! Fucking and oral sex are the only talents I possess. Since my first time with a woman, I have known that I have an amazing talent for pleasing the opposite sex.

S.H.E. Robot

This is going to be possibly the best day of my life. I am so excited I can hardly fucking stand it. This past year, I have made a series of films that have brought in tons of money and most of it came straight to me. I have always wanted the perfect woman, so to speak. So I went out and bought one. It sounds unbelievable I know, but I am on my way to pick her up now. She cost me 250,000 bucks, but she will be worth it in my opinion. I have always wanted a robot, and when I heard about the new S.H.E. Robot, I couldn't resist. I read about her in a science magazine and knew I had to have one. She is supposed to be like having the perfect mate except you don't have to be faithful to her. If she gets on your nerves, you simply shut her off. How cool is that? I love women but I don't always want to listen to their constant complaints and demands. S.H.E. Robot sounds like the perfect mate for me. I can only imagine what the perfect woman must be like, but I intended to find out. Life is good.

I arrived at "Erotic Robotics" just in time to see my fantasy robot girl. I was so excited I could hardly get my seat belt off. I went inside, explained my reason for being there, sat down, and waited for Dr. Yang to emerge. About 10 minutes later, I saw him approach the row of seats where I was seated. He walked over to me and shook my hand. He escorted me back to a room full of robotic accessories. Dr. Yang went to the back and then shortly thereafter he emerged with my robot. My chin nearly dropped to the floor. She was absolutely smoking hot and then some!

She was everything I had ever dreamed about in a woman and more. It was hard to believe she was actually a robot. Her name is Callista and she has all of the features I had always found incredibly sexy in a woman. Her hair was a multitude of colors depending upon how the light hit it. It looked as though a rainbow of colors was caressing it and it shimmered like a million moonbeams. There were no words to describe it that would do it justice. She had the most beautiful hair I had ever seen. Her eyes were just as lovely. They glistened a mix of blue, green, and brown with flecks of gold interspersed. I had never in my life seen such radiant eyes. When Callista smiled, she lit up the room like rays of sunshine. She was the most brilliant and gorgeous woman I had ever laid eyes on. She literally took my breath away. If all of that was not enough, her body was even more spectacular. She stood about 5 feet 5 inches tall and had the most perfect legs. They were long, but not too long and very lean. I could imagine them up by my ears now as I fucked her pussy hard. The special thing about the S.H.E. Robot is the fact that they are programmed to be perfect in bed. They supposedly "learn" the preferences of the one they fuck and adjust their behavior to suit it. I could hardly wait to get her home and try out her sexual talents. I continued to check out every inch of her body as she smiled at me sexily. She had perfectly round tits and they looked to be the precise size that I had ordered, 34D. I was able to choose the features she would have and she turned out even more perfect than I had ever dreamed she would be.

I finally had the nerve to walk over to Callista and introduce myself. She seemed to be in love with me immediately. Technology amazed me. Who says money can't buy happiness? If it weren't for huge sums of money, I wouldn't be staring into the face of my dream woman right now. I went over a few technical details with Dr. Yang and then finally it was time to head home with Callista. I led her to my car and opened the door for her. It was amazing. No one would ever believe that she was a robot. She looked just like a real woman, only better. I could not believe how life-like she was.

We rode and talked. I told her a little bit about myself and she listened well. I had asked for a robot woman with an understanding and quieter personality. I could see they had listened and did what I had asked. Callista had such a quiet and sexy voice that I got a hard-on just listening to her talk as we drove toward my house. I could almost swear she was trying to make me horny. I noticed she kept looking down in her lap as if to look at something. Then, she would adjust something on her side. I envisioned her getting extremely wet and it made me rock-hard.

We finally made it to the house and I helped her out of the vehicle. She had a small bag with some belongings and a few clothes. I didn't know exactly what we would do when we got inside, but I assumed we would find something to do, if you know what I mean. We went inside and I told her to make herself comfortable. She was agreeable and then immediately got up and asked me what she could do for me. I was a bit alarmed because women I dated were not usually so agreeable. Before I could answer, Callista went around to my backside and started to massage my shoulders. It felt better than any massage I had ever had. Her hands felt like the hands of a Swedish masseuse kneading every sore muscle and causing my cock to become extremely erect.

It truly put me into ecstasy's grasp as she kneaded every muscle in my back. I swear her hands were magic and they felt completely human. I had a strong desire to turn around and kiss her passionately. This is exactly what I did too. I was kind of frightened about how it would be to kiss a robot but she felt incredibly natural. In fact, she had the softest lips I had ever had the pleasure of kissing. She seemed eager to kiss me back and she was the one who increased the intensity. She pulled me closer as if begging me to throw her on the bed and fuck her. I was getting hornier by the second, so I simply took her by the hand

and led her upstairs to the bed. I thought I would be in control, but I suddenly learned exactly what Callista was all about and what her greatest talent in the world was. I had met my match for sure.

Sex Goddess

Once we got to the bedroom, the real Callista came out. She began to undress seductively right before my eyes. I couldn't believe my eyes, her nude body was complete perfection. It blew me away with its beauty and appeal. She looked at me with animal desire and I walked over toward her. She unzipped my pants and took out my raging cock. It was hard as steel and in need of a good fuck. She pulled it out as if she had done it a thousand times and dropped to her knees and went down on me.

I almost fell to the ground she sucked it so well. It was the best blowjob I had ever received and this included the women in the porn flicks with me. I could not believe what I was feeling. Her mouth was the best feeling mouth that had ever wrapped its lips around my horny dick. She expertly licked up and down my horny shaft, paying close attention to the head and rim. I cannot even describe the feelings of nirvana I was catapulted into. She sucked as if she had been sucking cocks off for years. She could win the gold medal if there was an Olympic cock-sucking competition. That's how great it was.

Any man that let her suck his cock would easily agree with me when I said she was the best in the world and even the best on the planet. As she sucked, I couldn't resist twisting her nipples between my thumb and middle finger. I also couldn't help but wonder if her robot pussy was wet.

I guided her over to the bed so I could find out. I worked my fingers inside of her and I noticed it was pretty darn wet. It actually felt wetter than human pussy does. I kissed and sucked her tits and I noticed that when I did this her pussy became increasingly wet. It's as if my sucking triggered a response in her cunt. She started to moan in almost a purring like sound. It was one of the hottest moans I had ever heard. It made me want to slam my dick inside of her and fuck her so hard she'd tremble. Then she said, "Fuck me Robbie. I need to be fucked by you now!" That's all it took and I was going to anyway.

So I laid her back and slid my hard 9-inch prick deep inside her robot cunt. I couldn't believe it, but I was actually screwing robot pussy and it felt amazing. Her body moved perfectly in rhythm with mine. It was as if we were meant to fuck. I could see now why they asked me all of the questions that they did before I purchased Callista. They had actually designed her specifically for me. I felt like I was on top of the world. I could tell she was beginning to get close to an orgasm by the moans escaping her mouth. I loved those hot moans she had. It was one of the best things about her. As far as I could see, Callista was the perfect lover. I couldn't find one thing wrong with her.

She asked me if I would eat her pussy and I almost fell out. I couldn't believe she even knew about that. But I really don't know why I was so surprised. After all, she was the best cocksucker I had ever seen. So I went down on her delicious robot cunt. It tasted divine. It tasted better than divine. It was the best tasting pussy I had ever tasted. As far as I could tell, Callista was the best at everything sexual. Just as I was promised, my robot was the perfect lover and more. Callista started to thrust her hips upward toward my hungry mouth. I noticed she was starting to suck her own nipple, which sent waves of juice into my mouth and down my throat. The more she sucked, the more she came and then she hollered one loud scream. A gush of pussy cum flooded my mouth and it was almost too much for me to take. She came more than any human female I had ever known. Dr. Yang had said they were able to design and program a robot that could emit bodily fluids unlike anything the world had ever seen, and he wasn't kidding. After making her cum so hard, Callista latched onto my dick and didn't let up until I squirted all over her face and down her throat. I could tell that she was bound and determined to drink every drop of my wanton cock bone dry. She was absolutely blowing my mind and I didn't think that was even possible.

Even the porno flicks I was in were never this fucking hot! I started to feel my balls stiffen and become giant receptacles of creamy dick cum. My big cock started to squirt like a volcanic eruption pulsating from my purple dick head. I groaned so loudly even I was shocked at the sounds escaping my mouth. It kept spewing as if my cock would never stop. I pushed her head down harder and harder, plunging deep within her throat with every ounce of strength I had. This hot robot had me beside myself with desire and horniness. I was quickly beginning to realize that she was well worth the $250,000 I spent on her. I swear it seemed like I came for a solid 15 minutes. I actually don't remember too much after that cumming experience. I fell fast asleep in blissful dreamland.

Dream Woman

The next morning I woke up to the smell of fresh bacon cooking and coffee brewing. Once the aroma entered my nostrils, I was wide-awake and wondering who was doing it. Oh yeah! I thought...Callista. I couldn't believe it that I had gotten so lucky that my robot woman was a cook too! I guess they truly listened to the personal requests I had about what I wanted in a woman.

I made my way downstairs and Callista turned to me and said "Good morning, Robbie. How do you take your coffee?"

"Cream and sugar," I said, and when she turned her back to me, I grabbed her from behind and kissed her neck. She turned around to face me and she greedily kissed me back with hot and horny desire written all over her kiss and her face. I squeezed her tight ass and noticed it was soft and pliable even more than you would ever think it could be. It was almost impossible to tell that Callista was a robot. She was so life-like it was totally unbelievable. It seems as well that my robot girl wakes up horny and I definitely like that a lot.

As she began to kiss me more hungrily, I noticed she was pressing her robot cunt into my crotch and causing my hard muscle to stand straight up. Fuck! I needed to let this dick go and get back inside of her hungry snatch. I cleared the dishes out of the way and took her right there on the kitchen table in front of our big picture window. I just hoped a horny neighbor would walk by and see me plowing this goddess for all it was worth. She could take dick hard and she could take cock fast. It didn't seem to matter how strong I plunged, she took it and seemed to be glad to do so. She was a fucking machine like no other woman had ever seen. She was by far the best fuck I had ever had!

On the Set

I had a taping to do that day on the porn set out in Malibu. It suddenly dawned on me, maybe Callista would like to come along and see what is involved in filming a porno. I asked her and she said okay. I waited a bit for her to get ready and then she came down looking hot enough to fucking eat. She had on a black mini dress and black stilettos. She was one sexy babe in that outfit. I kissed her once again and then ran 3 of my fingers inside her hot wet cunt and she moaned. I swear it actually sounded like she squirted a bit. She got so incredibly wet it threw me a bit every time I felt it. I tasted her upon my fingers and then she grabbed my fingers for a taste of her squirt too. That was so fucking hot!

I would have loved to screw her, but I had to get to the set of my new porno flick. We raced down the interstate toward the studio. She stroked my cock the whole way getting me ready for my filming I suppose. I was always horny, so there wasn't an issue with me not being hard. We got to the set just in time. I introduced Callista to everyone including my two main costars Crystal Falls and Candy Lips. They were nice enough to Callista, but I detected a hint of jealousy among the ladies. I told them that there were plenty of the Robbie Grinders to go around and they should not worry. All 3 rolled their eyes simultaneously.

I let Callista know where she could sit while we taped some of the scenes, and I told her to feel free to get look around or get a snack or whatever she needed to do while we shot scenes. We started our first hard-core scene and I tried my best to keep an eye on Callista off to the side. I noticed she was being rather quiet at first but then suddenly I noticed Callista doing something rather shocking but still very naughty. She started to masturbate while watching me pound these two babes into the headboard. I was so intrigued by her masturbation that was so openly blatant that I damn near forgot the movie I was making until Crystal elbowed me and got me back on track. So I rejoined my snatch-eating babes until I made Crystal shoot a squirt 2 feet up in the air and splash me down, soaking me big time! Crystal was one hot tamale, but I had an idea that Callista could probably out-shoot her any day when it came to pussy squirts. I then started plowing Candy's big pussy hard and fervently. While I plowed her cunt, Crystal brought hers right over to my mouth and stuck her bush right in my face. Fuck, I loved my job!

When that happened, I took a look at Callista and saw she was spread eagle fingering the fuck out of her robot hole. She turned me on so much I unloaded my spunk deep into Candy's canal. Callista had a way of getting to me like no other woman ever had. I was planning on keeping that little bit of information a secret. I yanked my muscle from Candy's pink cunt and Crystal immediately slapped my dick down her throat. It was quite a turn-on to yank your cock from a pussy to a hot porn queen's mouth in 2 seconds flat. I noticed some of the set guys and the grips were getting into Callista's masturbatory show a little too much. A couple of them even had their dicks poking out of their zippers wanking off at the same time that they watched my robot chick.

That's when I decided to stop filming and try something totally out of the blue. I walked over to Callista and asked her if she would like to have a part in our movie. She perked up like a schoolgirl at a Friday night football game. "Sure I'd love that, Robbie!" and she wrapped her arms tightly around my neck and gave me a huge hug. I heard sighs from behind me and I could see that Crystal and Candy were not liking the idea of Callista being a part of our raunchy flick one bit. "Ladies, let's please try to get along like good girls okay?" They all shook their heads, but very begrudgingly so.

Callista walked close to me, gave me a huge French kiss, then dropped to her knees, and started sucking my cock very hard and deep. I told Callista it was time to start shooting the film and informed her that she wouldn't be in it for about 10 minutes more so to step aside until called on the set. She looked kind of pissed, but she did as I said.

When the tape rolled again, it was time for Crystal to close with a big POV-style blowjob scene with me. Crystal always did extremely well with these. During the BJ, Callista and Candy were scheduled to enter the set and be eating each other's cunts out. Callista walked onto the set and put on the best performance any one had ever seen from a porn star or goddess of her caliber. She was a natural in front of the camera and she literally made Crystal and Candy seem insignificant. She illuminated when she was having sex and especially when she knew she was on film. Her appearance became almost iridescent. Her hair even took on a rainbow glow like it did the day I picked her up and took her home.

I kept my purchase of Callista a secret and it was quite a trip that she was able to fool people. It was easy to see that they didn't have the slightest clue that Callista was made of metal and computer parts. All that I cared about were the blowjobs that I was receiving by her robotic highness. It was spectacular and I didn't even have to act or be the womanizing Robbie Grinder. It was very possible that this robot babe was going to change me. If sex with her continued to be such an amazing experience, I don't see why I would ever need a woman other than my sweet Callista.

I had to pinch myself to see if this was really me talking. "Robbie Grinder never gets serious with a woman, much less a robot," I told myself time and time again. I couldn't help it; Callista had a spell on me that wasn't going to end in a few seconds. I finally reclined back in a chair and watched this dazzling cosmic cutie go to work on me. She did it all. She performed every single act that any man would agree is definitely in the top 10 turn-ons. She even stuck her ass way out in the air while she had me buried once gain balls deep. Fuck! I thought she was going to suckle my meat into a spunkilicious cum fiesta. She had my experienced shaft shivering and my head was having a heyday. If this is what my dick was in for, then I never wanted it to stop. On top of that, Callista was officially my new costar. I bet she and I are going to be millionaires before too long. To end our sexual frenzy, Callista and I got into the 69 position and put on a wild performance for our audience. But it wasn't a performance in my book. It was the real thing. I was in paradise and I never intended to let it stop.

Callista and I had an amazing future ahead of us, I could feel it, and I am pretty sure she could too. We ended the movie with a bang, so to speak. Callista did beat Crystal in the competition of pussy squirting, and she shot about 3 feet high and opened her robot pussy wide for all to enjoy as it oozed the most glimmering cum I had ever seen. That may well be the best scene that has ever been shot in the name of porn. I was one happy porn star, and from the looks of it, Callista was pretty darn ecstatic herself. She and I had met our match in each other, and in my opinion, the sky was the limit for us. There was absolutely nothing she and I couldn't do together in the genre of sex and erotica. We would take our rightful places as the king and queen of porn one day very soon.

2 NAUGHTY RICH GIRL 1

Daddy's Little Rebel

"Charlotte! I need to speak with you immediately; come down here!" yells my overzealous and annoying daddy. I am so tired of jumping to his every demand. I cannot wait until I go off to college in a few months. My daddy is overprotective and hardheaded. He's a filthy rich Mississippi businessman who tries to control everybody, including me. My name is Charlotte Montgomery and my dad is a rich tycoon known well around these parts, named Charles Montgomery.

We live in a huge mansion outside of Biloxi, Mississippi, that used to belong to some general in the war a zillion years ago. I love the money and the stuff that comes along with being filthy rich, but I am a free spirit at heart and I desire to do something wild and free that my daddy would hate. One day I am going to do it so my daddy will learn his lesson about controlling me, once and for all. My mama died of cancer when I was 8, so daddy is super protective of me. I love him, but I am sick of his rules. I just turned 18, so I figure anything I want to do will have to be okay with him. I'm legal now.

I galloped downstairs to see what on earth my daddy was hollering about.

"What is it daddy?" I said.

"I want you to stay out of the yard and away from the pool area today, you hear me Charlotte?"

"Yes, I hear you, but what on earth for?" I replied sarcastically.

"The hired help will be working today and maybe even for a week or more on the grounds and on the pool in preparation for your going away party. I have to go to Atlanta on business so I expect you to behave yourself for the 3 or 4 days that I am away," said daddy sternly.

"I am not a 3-year-old daddy," I replied. "I am 18 now and a woman." Daddy gave me one of his warning looks and doled out about 10 other rules for me to follow that I planned on breaking the minute he drove away. He left our housekeeper Tillie in charge, but she and I were tight. Tillie always let me do what I wanted. She loved and trusted me. I always let her take off early and go home to her family when daddy went on business trips. I always gave her an extra hundred out of my allowance to keep my secrets too. Sometimes I even let her borrow my platinum card overnight if I really wanted her to stay quiet.

I felt particularly rebellious this time so I

gave her 2 hundred and 2 credit cards. As soon as daddy was well out of sight, I drove Tillie home and told her to come in late the next day if she wanted. She was all smiles when she got out of my red convertible. I was free and it felt good, so I drove 90 all the way back to the mansion. I also picked up 2 packs of Virginia Slim cigarettes on the way home and a bottle of champagne. I was going to get fried out by the pool and daddy couldn't stop me. I lit up my first cigarette and contemplated the fun I was going to have. I was going to get some cock while daddy was gone, I knew that much! I hadn't been fucked in a month and I was extremely horny. Daddy had loomed over me so much I hadn't even had the chance to play with my cunt toys.

Daddy's Naughty Nympho

Before I even got back to the mansion I had my mini skirt hiked up and was fingering my slit with my left index finger. I am basically a horny little nympho 24/7. Daddy would probably croak if he knew, but he doesn't. I've always screwed older guys so they would keep my secret. I had already screwed probably 8 men this year. I always took my birth control pill and made them use rubbers. I could even slip one on a cock with my teeth.

I was starting to get wet as fuck so I slipped the champagne bottle inside my hungry cunt. I fucked myself with the neck until I was about to have a hot orgasm, then I quit. There was an intersection coming up and I hoped a car with a horny man in it would stop beside me so I could masturbate for him. I might even fuck my stick shift if he's lucky.

One time I was fucking myself with my hairbrush and daddy pulled up. I barely got the brush out and my cunt covered before he came in. The weird thing is that I had started my orgasm so I had to keep having it. So I looked at him and waved trying to hide the very sexy and hot look that I am sure was all over my face. When he finally left again I squirted my pussy so hard it splashed onto my arms. One more second and daddy would have seen me gush.

I let out a moan that was uncontainable and I pulled over to finish my snatch off. I also had the talent of eating my own pussy off. That was a talent I had to save for the house though. I have always been involved in ballet so I could easily stretch my body where I could reach my own pussy. It felt more amazing than anything on earth too!

I finally pulled up to the mansion. I raced inside and put on my crotchless thong. I left my tits topless. I grabbed my bottle of bubbly, my cigs, and my favorite wand vibe. I also grabbed a tube of lubricant on the way out and a towel. I barely made it down to the pool without dropping my various sundry items. I heard daddy's voice echoing through my head but I didn't care! I wanted to enjoy the pool and get my ass tanned. I am a self-proclaimed little nympho and damn proud of it. I see absolutely nothing wrong with wanting to fuck anything that moves. I had even gotten my best gal pal Veronica into finger fucking me and letting me do her. Next time I plan on eating her cunt out. I did her with four fingers last time, and she blasted white girl spunk everywhere. I even licked some of it up and she squirted again. It was damn hot. I had popped my cork on my champagne bottle while inside and I had to go back inside to fetch my tunes and my tanning oil.

I made my way back out by the pool and lit a Virginia Slims as I poured myself a wine glass full of bubbly. Then I put oil all over my exposed places, which was just about every place on my horny body. I should use sunscreen because I am light blonde headed and fair skinned. I sure didn't want to mess up my tan with a sunburn. The lobster look had a way of ruining a nice golden tan, in my opinion.

I was so intent on what I was doing and on pampering my body that I didn't notice the stranger until I looked up. When I finally decided to look up and get my mind off of my crotch for a second, I saw his very sexy and fine ass looking at me like he'd love to attack my cunt right that second with his hungry mouth. I assumed he was the hired help daddy had spoken about, but there was only one thing wrong with this picture and with the fairy tale in my mind, the man was black. My dad would never want me to sunbathe in front of any man and, because he is very racist, especially not a black man.

Daddy's Little Sex Pot

I smiled sexily at the black godlike creature standing before me. He was so hot, and he had a rock-hard muscled body to die for. I would have to be out of my mind not to be attracted to this man. He reached out his hand and introduced himself: "Hi, my name is Marcus Wilson. It is nice to meet you."

I replied, "Hi, my name is Charlotte Montgomery, and the pleasure is completely mine." I flirted with my best charm and sex appeal that I knew how to. I suddenly remembered that I was topless and I had my crotchless undies on. I guess that kind of leaves out the possibility of leaving something to the imagination.

Marcus and I chatted a bit and then he explained that he needed to get back to work on our grounds and on the pool. I didn't like that one bit. I felt as though he needed to be pointing all of his attention, and his cock, directly at me. I could tell I turned him on big time. I could see the bulge in his shorts get a little bigger while he tried not to stare at my big pink cunt lips. But I knew he was just dying to get his mouth on them and suck so hard and so long that my body quivered in ecstasy. I decided it was time to perform for Marcus a little bit. He needed to see what it really felt like to go wild with need and fervent desire.

While Marcus went to work cleaning our pool, I decided to put on a hot little show. I retreated inside the mansion for a while and changed into my pink and black polka dot bikini that I looked amazingly hot in. I also got my boom box so I could have some tunes while I danced and turned Marcus on big time! I then sauntered my sexy ass back outdoors. I laid down sexily in my chaise lounge and seductively I began fingering my hot cunt. I could see out of the corner of my eye that Marcus was keeping a pretty close eye on my little "dance."

In fact, a few times he looked at me like he might just walk over, strip me nude, and fuck me. I had no problem with that if he wanted to, that's for sure! I slowly stripped my own bikini top revealing my perky tits to Marcus. He may well be the sexiest black man I have ever laid eyes on, I thought to myself while I fingered my clit furiously. As he watched me finger fuck my hole, I saw him inadvertently grab and "adjust" his black dick, which seemed to be getting pretty damn big in his shorts by this time. I could tell he wanted to jerk on his black snake so bad he could taste it. I very badly wanted to see him reveal his huge muscle too.

I needed to be fucked in the worst way, and Marcus looked like he could oblige me in that quite well. His dick kept growing as I kept toying with my pussy like a wild woman. As I got up on all fours and gave him a bird's eye view of my snatch, I couldn't help but wonder how well Marcus ate out pussy. As I continued to perform for Marcus, I noticed he was coming closer and closer over to where I was. I could tell it wouldn't be much longer and he'd be banging my white cunt like nobody's business.

I kept fingering and he kept inching closer and closer until he was standing only about 2 feet away from me. That's when Marcus chose to reveal his huge dick to me. I almost gushed on the spot when I saw his ample cock. The girth of it alone was about like a pop can. I had fucked some big cocks but none of them were ever this big. I was in awe of his dick and couldn't wait to feel it thrust inside me. He grabbed the massive rod and started stroking it ever so slowly. This made me want to gush instantly. His hands on his cock looked so fucking good I could hardly take it. As he stroked his black dick, I mimicked his actions with a stroke on my clit and then my lips. We stood face to face in mutual masturbatory delight.

Out of the blue Marcus started to jerk his huge cock fast and furiously. I repeated the furious motion by strumming my clit. The harder he jerked, the faster I flicked. I was kind of surprised when suddenly Marcus said, "Lie down on your chaise lounge; I want to eat the fuck out of your cunt." I was never one to argue so I did as Marcus requested. Before he even touched his hot lips to my throbbing cunt, he licked my inner thighs until I shivered even in the summer sun. Fuck, he was such a turn on! I was definitely ready to be eaten out and screwed hard. He made his way to my snatch and breathed his warm air all over my hungry cunt.

"Eat my fucking naughty pussy, baby," I said to him. When I said that, I meant for him to get after my pussy like he had never done before. I was raging horny and not about to stop being that way until this naughty cunt of mine is satisfied. The way Marcus Wilson ate a pussy is almost impossible to describe, it was so damn hot. He slowly but surely took each of my pussy lips one at a time suckling and tasting them tenderly. He definitely took his sweet time with a cunt and I loved that. Every lick and every lap had me nearly screaming in red-hot ecstasy.

He spent a long while simply enjoying my labia and all of her folds. He lapped seductively and licked playfully. He definitely knew his way around a cunt. I bucked my ass and whole body upwards towards his greedy mouth and lips not wanting him to stop his feasting on my wet pussy. It had been a while since I was fucking eaten out, and I was fervent as hell.

After he tantalized my juicy cunt lips until I thought I'd bust a nut, he started in on the rest of my snatch. He was the best pussy eater I had ever encountered, bar none! He ate me so damn good I had to hold back my squirt. That's when I decided to show him my very own talent because I was hungry for my own cunt. I told him to grab his black snake and start wanking while he watched my performance. I drew my legs up over my head and then behind me on the towel I was laying on. I then went to town on my throbbing cunt lips. I lapped each one painstakingly slow, drawing each one out of my mouth's grasp ever so seductively. My body couldn't help but jerk from the pre-orgasmic cramps I was experiencing. I absolutely got off on my own pussy, that's all there was to it. It felt like every drop of cum in my body was on the edge of soaking my pouty mouth.

It tasted like honey and strawberry elixir, and if I ate on it too long, I'd squirt all over my own face. I knew I was getting to that point so to end my nasty little show I drew my left lip out as long as I could and then released it in a snap. Marcus almost blew his wad when I did that. It was naughty, I must admit. I was surprised he was able to hold his cum load but he was. He was stroking his black cock so hard though, the head was a plum color and throbbing. It looked naughty as fuck as he stroked up and down the lengthy shaft. Before I realized what he was going to do with that black meat, he plunged it down my throat. I was shocked but pleased. His black dick cum tasted amazing and it tasted different than white cock cream. I wanted to savor every last drop of it. I licked it on the end of my tongue and let Marcus see his cream in my mouth, and I so craved the taste of my girl goo.

I could see his big black balls drawing up hard like he was ready to bust a nut. I have never seen a dick so fucking stiff and raging in my life. I couldn't wait for him to slam it in my cunt like he did my mouth. I sucked and licked his raging dark meat for a while longer while Marcus groaned and pushed my head down harder onto his cock. I gagged, and I am sure my eyes bulged as he buried his hard-on deep down my hungry throat. I could taste precum increasing the more I nursed his cunt teaser. My cunt runneth over with the notion of what he would feel like buried in my hungry snatch. His cockhead tasted like an angry demand urgently needing to be pacified.

My clit felt like a million pinpricks waiting to slide up along the shaft of his swollen implement. I could hardly keep from squirming as I sucked his black wand; I was so damn turned on. I was practically bucking like a bronco wanting to get screwed really badly!

Marcus must have read my dirty mind because he asked if we could go inside and fuck. I said of course, obviously, and led him upstairs to my bedroom. I slipped my towel off sexily and lay down on my purple satin bedspread. Marcus removed his pants, revealing his huge dick in all of its massive glory. It was one of the best-looking cocks I had ever seen, and I almost drooled looking at it. I motioned to the hunk to join me on my bed of lust. He obliged of course.

He took my legs and positioned them spread-eagle out to each side as he prepared my cunt for his girth. I moaned in sheer ecstasy. I was so fucking turned on I could hardly take the torture anymore. I wanted to get fucked, and I wanted to get fucked right this minute! I was burning inside to be screwed. He took his right hand and stroked his black dick as long as he could possibly get it and then slowly, inch by excruciating inch, guided that big cock inside my flaming cunt hole. I practically screamed; it felt so fucking hot when he first entered my horny pussy.

Marcus continued holding my trembling legs out to the side, just daring me to try and escape his big meat. While he continued to, inch by inch, screw me, he reached down and nursed my horny tits. They were pink, puffy, and about to burst; I was so hot and turned the fuck on. He'd suck hard as hell, then let up, and flick the nipple end with his tongue, sending waves of ecstasy through my turned on body. His mouth would mimic his cock's actions to a tee. This was the best sex I had ever had, without a doubt.

The more we fucked, the more I wanted him inside me. He then asked me to roll over so he could hammer me doggie style. Marcus said he intended to fuck me in every position known to mankind and then do it again the next day. I was thrilled by the whole idea, believe me. I flipped over, stuck my tight ass right out in the air, and put my hairless pussy on display for Marcus to drool over and bang the fuck out of.

He grabbed my hair from behind and balled it in his fist and then Marcus started to bang me. It felt awesome as he plunged in and then out and then in again. He'd fuck it slow and then suddenly increase his speed to a fast and furious level that had my pussy throbbing and aching. He was screwing me to the wall and then some! Actually, he did bang me hard, standing up. He picked me up and I wrapped my legs around his strong hips. He held me up while he pounded my cunt like nine ways to Sunday. He leaned me against the wall and pounded me even harder and French kissed my mouth and tits while he did it.

I felt my pussy lips tightening their grip around Marcus's swollen dick. I knew I was about to squirt my wads everywhere, and I felt his balls tighten close to the base of my cunt. I knew he was about to shoot. I decided I wanted to ride him and we would come together that way. He was agreeable, and we went to my purple satin bed. I got on top of him and lowered my pussy ever so slowly down upon his cock. I rocked gently back and forth on it, making sure to feel and savor every last inch of his amazing dick.

This was the best cock I had ever sat on, and I wanted to relish every drop of him and his cum. I ground my hips in seductive figure eights. He reached up with fingertips, squeezed my hard-as-rock nipples, while I threw my head back, and enjoyed the feast my pussy was having. I rocked and squirmed all over Marcus's cock until I felt the gushes coming and coming strong. The scent of animal lust engulfed the room and seemed to hang like curtains all around us. It was almost as if I had been lifted into a vacuum of sheer ecstasy. Everything around us seemingly disappeared. As my orgasm began, my whole body started to tremble from head to toe. I was lost in a place between earth and paradise. I could feel every pore on my body, yet everything was numb like I had been ingesting some powerful narcotic. I never wanted this feeling to end. It was erotic and explosive and the best I had ever felt in my entire life. And in between breaths was where the fire seemed to hurt the most. I needed my sanity back, the sanity from an orgasm to rip me back to reality.

I needed the climactic and earth shattering release, yet I wanted to dangle right here in this heavenly seduction. Every single inch of my body felt ready to explode...the tingles turned into dull roars as my flesh awoke to a sense of passion I have rarely ever felt before. I knew my body, and I knew what we would share would be earthshattering. Every single inch of me stood erect from my hair on my head down to balls of my feet.

This is the point my fucking cunt began to expel its juices. I gushed all over his angry meat. I felt my pussy lips clamp in a dead lock around his girth. They seemed to have a chokehold, and I wondered if he'd get stuck in me like some savage beast. In the midst of my near outer body experience of an orgasm, Marcus's dick stood high and proud like a soldier and started to pop off. He grunted a big throaty animal grunt, and I again wondered whether he would be stuck in me for the remainder of the night. As he started to spew, he groped my hard tits for all they were worth. For a moment, I thought my nips might just squirt cum.

Marcus unloaded every last drop within me, and my pussy had him in a vice grip that he wouldn't soon forget. We finally collapsed in a spent heap on my silk sheets, staring at each other in wonderment. We were complete strangers a few hours earlier now that we had experienced some intense and intimate moments, for damn sure. I looked at him and told him how fucking hot it was and how much he turned me on. He told me he felt what we shared was merely the beginning of one taboo affair that was only going to get better. Then I thought of my very racist daddy. He would kill me, but that is only if he found out. I knew Marcus and I had a few more days to experience one another. I decided to call Tillie and give her the next day off. Marcus and I went outside and worked together until dark. I invited him to spend the evening with me and he said yes. As we ate dinner, I thought about how much this black man turned me on and how much I already wanted his cock inside me again. I was going to take it very soon. What daddy didn't know couldn't hurt him.

3 NAUGHTY RICH GIRL 2

Daddy's Kinky Girl

After one night with Marcus Wilson, I was completely hooked on his hot body and kinky ways. My very controlling and racist father was still out of town. While he was away in Atlanta on business, I intended to play house with Marcus. My daddy is a filthy rich Mississippi businessman, and he hired Marcus to do some work on our pool and our grounds. Of course, Daddy told me to stay away from Marcus, but I never mind him. I am 18 now anyway and free to do what I want with my body and my mind in my own humble opinion.

My daddy left our maid Tillie in charge to watch out for me, but I had given her the last 2 days off with one of my credit cards and 200 bucks to keep quiet. Doing those things usually kept Tillie quiet and they kept me fucked. I was horny damn near constantly and

Marcus had a huge black dick that satisfied the fuck out of me. He had to run home to shower and change, but I couldn't wait until he returned and we could do some more nasty.

He had plenty of hard cock to satisfy me, and he was just kinky and "bad boy" enough to keep me interested. In fact, I had a few surprises in store for Marcus today when he returned. I was absolutely excited about it and I couldn't wait. I needed to make a phone call to square the deal.

Round Two

While I waited for Marcus to get back to the mansion, I showered and put on my hot little red dress. I did my hair kind of wild and sexy so Marcus could run his fingers through it while he fucked me hard. I needed sex and I needed it now. Marcus called me up on his cell phone and said he would be here soon. I was ecstatic. I couldn't wait to see his sexy black ass again!

Just when I was thinking about fingering myself off thinking about Marcus, I heard him pull up outside. I ran like a crazy chick outside to greet his fine self. I ran to Marcus and threw my arms around him while at the same time I gave him the hottest and most intense French kiss he had probably ever received. He returned the kiss with amazing fervency. I immediately got wet as hell down south and could feel my cunt lips throbbing. I led him inside the mansion with one hand. The second I closed the door behind us, Marcus unleashed his beast-like passion upon me.

He attacked me with an intensity so strong even I was stunned by it. I have never had a man who wanted me as badly as Marcus Wilson did. He was a one-man sex machine. He knew all of the right moves to make my body shiver and yearn for more. I took him by the hand and led him over to our kitchen table, which had a huge picture window right behind it. I have always wanted to almost get caught fucking. The thought of it truly turned me on. I dropped my little red dress to the floor, hopped up onto the kitchen table and said to Marcus, "Eat me out right now here on the kitchen table!" Marcus smiled and immediately dove between my legs and latched onto my raging cunt.

"Mmmm fuck." I moaned animal-like and with a desperation in my voice that exuded lascivious need.

Marcus groaned with a mouthful of love box and wallowed full force between my thighs and pussy lips. He took his time and made sure his tongue and mouth didn't miss one spot upon my hot and writhing snatch. His tongue felt like a luxurious hot, moist toy playing my pussy like a virtuoso with a bow on a violin. His tongue caressed each fold to sheer perfection. Marcus was partaking of my pounding and gushing snatch like he was the expert extraordinaire when it came to cunnilingus.

I spread my long legs as far as I possibly could. I did this to ensure that Marcus's tongue and mouth had a full access to ensure he would reach me with his full mouth and ever-sexy tongue. He paced sweet kisses here and there in between suckles and plunges and then he decided it was time to watch and flick a little bit of my own pussy off again.

I must admit, I was oozing cream just thinking of tasting my own snatch and flicking my tongue against my hard as a rock clit. I got in my self-pussy eating position and went to town on my naughty snatch.

It felt so fucking good running my wet juicy tongue all over my own clit head. I loved flicking my tongue all over the slippery end of my horny love button. I also got off seeing I was turning Marcus the fuck on while he watched me eat myself out. I had to put my legs behind my ears and it was ultra-nasty just barely being able to touch my clit with my hungry mouth.

I wanted to eat it harder and harder the closer I got to making my clit cum like mad. It tingled underneath my tongue tip and the very end of my tongue was hard as a rock, as was my horny button. I started to jerk and tremble all over my body by this time. I could see Marcus out of my peripheral vision jerking the fuck out of his cock. I was really getting into my self-eating private show when I suddenly remembered the phone call I had made that morning before Marcus showed up. I smiled with pussy in my mouth and Marcus about busted a nut right then and there.

Two For One

I decided now was as good of a time as any to tease the absolute shit out of Marcus Wilson. Of course, he'd love to see me make myself cum, but I had some hot plans for him. Little did he know that earlier that morning I had phoned my best girlfriend Veronica. She and I had played around a few times before, and I absolutely loved her naughty snatch. She had a full-grown bush and it was black and silky. It was just the opposite of my blonde, nearly bald peach fuzz. Marcus had a real decadent treat in store for him. He was soon going to get the best of both worlds. Veronica and I had a very naughty threesome in store for sexy Marcus Wilson. Just when I had my mind all covered and creamed with Veronica's cunt, the phone rang and it was Daddy. Fuck! I thought but I had to answer the call. Marcus being the bad boy that he is, fingered my sloppy cunt while I talked to Daddy. It was all that I could do not to cream right then and there and moan out loud.

I finally got my daddy off the phone. It was good I answered though, because he informed me he would be home in about 3 days. That gave me and Marcus plenty of time to do the nasty. I was trying to keep Marcus occupied until we heard the familiar bell at the door. It was familiar to me, but it was going to be a surprise to Marcus.

Just when I thought I'd go fucking crazy with anticipation the doorbell rang. It was kind of funny because Marcus's eyes nearly popped out of his head. I went over, gave him a quick peck, and said "Poor baby. Don't be scared. I am sure it's nobody."

"Charlotte, what are you up to?" Marcus replied suspiciously.

I didn't answer and walked to the French

doors and swung them open.

"Veronica!" I proclaimed with schoolgirl glee. "Charlotte!" Veronica replied with as much enthusiasm and then threw her arms around me. We kissed opposing cheeks like proper rich girls and then bumped crotches like improper rich girls. I grabbed my best friend ever by the hand and said, "Veronica, I would like you to meet Marcus."

"The pleasure is all mines I am sure," said Veronica in an almost purring sound sizing Marcus up like a lion-sized up a zebra in Africa. I swear she even paused at his cock a whole 20 seconds. She was shameless! And I loved her for it!

Marcus extended his big hand to Veronica and then he kissed the top of her hand sending her swooning into next week. I made a gagging noise and then invited the two of them over to the bar for a drink or a beer from the fridge. The three of us deciding on Coronas with lime and then sat down in our comfy but spacious living room. The deep mahogany wood and the burgundy furniture seemed to add to the sexual ambience in the air.

We were quietly sipping our beers when Marcus and I both distinctly hear a buzzing noise. It didn't take long to figure out that it was coming from Veronica's body or something. I out my hand to my mouth and chuckled and Veronica shot us that look she has. Veronica is a knockout; there is no doubt about it. She and I are both pretty hot actually but opposites in the looks department.

I have long blonde, almost towhead, curls

and a petite frame and I am only 5 foot 2 inches with heels. Veronica is at least 5 foot 6 inches, log silky black hair, and olive skinned. She also has deep green smoldering eyes that drive the boys/men bananas. I have pale ocean blue eyes. Veronica and I always were a pair growing up. Guys looked at it like they were getting the best of both worlds.

I regressed thinking back but the buzzing noise that was most definitely emerging from Veronica's crotch seemed to be intensifying. Just like the typical horny dude, Marcus's hand headed directly for his dick to do some last minute adjustments. In other words, he had to cop a feel of his quickly stiffening rod of destruction. I must admit hearing the buzz was getting my cunt all hot and bothered as well. I wished she had brought me one but of course, I had mine in my nightstand if I just had to whip out the vibes and the dongs.

I must admit the more I thought about Veronica running around all morning with a vibe stuck up her cunt, the hornier I got. It was quite an erotic turn on to say the least. Veronica had an amazing cunt. I could say so from experience. I was bit worried that Marcus might actually gravitate to her pussy after he tried it out. But I refused to let my mind travel down that jealous road. We had a threesome to get to.

I looked over and noticed that Marcus was wanking away at his black cock harder now. I also noticed Veronica doing a little trick with her vibe. She'd thrust it in and out of her pussy kind of like a now you see it now you don't type thing. In fact, you could even liken her wanton snatch to a jack in the box the way she popped that vibe in and out of her so sexily.

I really couldn't take Veronica's naughty little ball busting game anymore so I shocked both her and Marcus, and I dove onto her cunt so fast she never saw it coming. The surprised look on both of their faces made my pussy swim in its own juice I swear it did! As I hungrily feasted on Veronica's hairy muff, Marcus came up behind me and stuck 3 fingers inside my greedy cunt. I bounced my ass back into his hand and took a firm suck and pull on Veronica's earlier vibe stuffed peach.

Veronica writhed in red-hot pleasure and bucked upwards towards my mouth. If Marcus were to keep up his finger fucking like he was doing, I was going cream on his black fingers for sure. I decided it was time for some switching around. I wanted to eat myself while I watched Veronica and Marcus fuck.

Two For One Special

I laid back in my one and only eat myself off position. Marcus had to take a look and I knew he would. That pleased me immensely. I absolutely loved making him hot as hell. As I put the end of my tongue to my clit, Marcus and Veronica looked on as if they wanted to cream instantly. It didn't matter how many times either of them had seen me do this; it was a unique talent that made others hot and horny. Veronica had tried several times to force her mouth to get into the position (and her body) to make herself cum but she couldn't.

As I was saying, at nearly the precise second that I made my own clit throb and jerk, Marcus entered Veronica doggie style. I strained my eyes just as hard as I could to see the two of them while still managing to flick the fuck out of my own pussy's lips and clit. It seemed as if simultaneously we all three let out one big "Mmmmmmm." We were all in sexual bliss it was easy to decipher. My pussy had never felt so much sweet nirvana, I am certain.

I could tell that even with her vast experience with being thrust hard by excited harder than rock dicks, Veronica was feeling pretty damn full by now. Marcus had pop can size girth. Even for the most seasoned fucker, it was a tough one to take all in one gigantic thrust. Veronica couldn't help but squirm and thrust her perfectly tight and round ass back towards Marcus as he plunged even deeper still.

It didn't take long before Veronica was digging his cock rhythm and she started to plow him actually. She pounded her big pussy back towards his throbbing cock. Bang, bang, bang went her luscious lips against his girth wrapping around Marcus even tighter than Veronica knew her pussy could. He felt so fucking good to her I could read her expression as if I was feeling it right along with her.

She motioned with her deep eyes for me to come over to where they were. Her expression was saying to me, "Come over here and suck my pussy cream off of your boyfriend's cunt teaser." Who was I to refuse my best friend such an important request? So that's what I did. I made my way over to Veronica and Marcus with my cunt lips flapping and my hole dripping. I didn't have time to think before Marcus plunged his big black wand down my hot throat. I noticed Veronica had her mini camcorder out trying to mimic the porno she had seen on OuiPorn probably the night before. She was addicted to porn and looked up to the stars. I felt my eyes bulge right out of their sockets, and Veronica said, "Make the gagging sound, Char. Come on!"

I could see that filming us was getting to her. She held the camera with one hand while her other was turning her cunt lips into a frothy blur. The deeper Marcus's cock went into my mouth and down my throat, the faster her fingers worked her succulent pussy. I could see her eyes going from the display screen of the camera to my eyes and then his cock. She squirmed as her fingers made her begin pumping her pussy against her frantic rubbing. Marcus looked back and forth from me to her and then down to my mouth.

This whole atmosphere was seedy but somehow electrically charged. I can feel the charge in the room. It felt like I did when I'd sneak candy from my mom's purse or when I was a teen I'd sneak off to the girl's room during math and finger the fuck out of cunt because my teacher gave me a clit hard-on. I would rush out the door like a prepubescent boy hoping no one saw my bulging clit sticking out. It was absolutely as hot as fuck what the three of us were doing and on the other hand, I wanted to scream. It smacked of love and all that good stuff. It truly spoke to me saying, "Charlotte, this seals it. You are a slutty bitch once and for all."

I would use my bulging clit like the cocks I had dreamed about for all of my life. I would grab it between my thumb and forefinger and jerk the fucker off until I creamed all over me, Veronica, or anyone else who happened to be in the way. My clit felt like a cock swollen so hard it would never go away. My pussy lips were spread open with desire, and my cream felt like molten honey as it dripped out of my sex-scented cave.

This is how I felt now. I wanted it to feel so fucking good yet so damn wrong. The very idea of doing something we shouldn't do is what drives many sex addicts. Then afterwards you feel like a complete piece of slutty trash, but it felt good at the time of mind numbing orgasm. I sucked, licked, probed, and nibbled my way up and down Marcus's rigid and purple shaft. I thought Marcus might just start convulsing. I looked up at him and he was so fucking hot he was unaware where the fuck he was. You could tell he felt so fucking horny it hurt. Then I suddenly did a knee jerk and damn near bit down too hard on Marcuse's bulbous prick head. Veronica sunk something deep inside my asshole, and it almost made my pussy squirt right then.

I didn't know which turned me on more, rubbing my own clit, watching Veronica rub hers, or knowing that Marcus was going to fill my throat with every drop of his thick hot spew. I was delirious with the excitement, frantic with my need, and determined that no matter what my cunt was going to cum hard, regardless of who did what to whom. It was a cluster fuck so to speak. We were all in a frenzy that couldn't be contained.

My eyes raced from here to there and every which way not knowing what to do. I was trying to consume every drop of this wild unadulterated sex the three of us were having. My hand went from clit to mouth to tit and back to lips. I was going nuts with wanton desire. You could cut the sexual tension in the air with a knife. It was electrical and energetic like some alien force. It was so charged up that Veronica made it clear that she wanted to have her turn nursing Marcuse's cock as well. I was agreeable to this because I wanted to eat out her cunt while she did this. We were like a three-person lust chain.

Marcus was leaning against a bar stool guiding Veronica's silky mane down onto his bulging, angry rod. Veronica had obviously seen too much porno by the gagging and fake slurping noises she made. I could help but smile like a Cheshire cat with a mouthful of delicious and almost fruity tasting muff. As I kneeled and took her fur delights on my knees, I worked my cunt hard with the vibe that started this sexual excursion about an hour earlier. I loved feasting on a pussy from behind. It tasted better somehow...if that was even possible.

I had never made it a secret that I enjoyed the fuck out of Veronica's naughty snatch. I ate it out now with a voracity likened to that of a hungry wolf. It was obvious by her bulging lips that kept trying to wrap themselves around my tongue that Veronica was on the verge of a squirt fiesta. The taste that was bursting from her pussy got stronger, and I began to lap lasciviously.

I looked up to see Marcus with his head thrown back and squinting his eyes in that pre-orgasm look that men often get. He suddenly started to form a low growl deep within his chest and exiting his mouth in an almost animal like roar. The look and sound of Marcus shooting his creamy hot load down my best friend's throat sent me reeling and bouncing underneath my own fingers. My lips swelled and wrapped around my fingers, and I suddenly inserted my fist into my own cunt and started to cum from the feel of my flapped out lips wrapped around my own wrist. I had always wanted to fist myself but had never been able to insert my whole fist inside my ample cunt until now. It felt so fucking hot I squirted all over my hand and I felt it dripping down my forearm.

I took my drenched fingers and stuck my cream up Veronica's aching pussy hole. She gasped and then squeezed and clenched her pussy around my three fingers so tightly I almost couldn't pull out. Then I felt Veronica start to gush her juicy cunt everywhere. I immediately dropped to my knees and started to drink her nectar. The taste alone made my pussy come again and again. There we were a three of us having a cum fest like none I had ever had before. It was the single most intense and erotic experience of my life. The sounds alone were such a huge turn on. Marcus was groaning like a caged beast, and Veronica and I had a moaning chorus going on that was pure sexual harmony. It seemed the three-way orgasm we had lasted a full 30 minutes although I am quite positive it didn't. That is just how exciting it was.

Not long afterwards Marcus and I saw Veronica outside to her candy apple red BMW. She gave us both a hug and a kiss and said we definitely needed to do this some other time. I looked at her and winked and then Marcus pinched her incredibly tight ass. One funny thing though, when I hugged Veronica I could still hear a slight buzz coming straight from Veronica's crotch. I chuckled to myself thinking what a nympho my best gal pal was! Even after at least 2 huge orgasms, her hot pussy was still aching to be satisfied. She might just be a bigger nympho than me, but I doubted that very seriously.

Marcus and I decided we had better do some of the chores my daddy had hired him to do before Marcus got in huge trouble. While we did yard work, I explained to Marcus about my daddy and how controlling and racist he is. Marcus said he thought he could handle my daddy, but I wasn't quite so sure. If he ever caught wind of any of this, he'd have my hide that's for sure. Of course, I had every intention of never letting big daddy ever find out about this at all. There was no reason at all that my hot, gorgeous, and extremely kinky new lover couldn't be my own dirty little secret. A girl has a right to a few secrets doesn't she? I figure that what Daddy doesn't know won't hurt him. Marcus was a hot as fuck lover, and I intended on keeping him no matter what Daddy thought and that was just how it was going to be. After all what could Daddy do about it anyway?

4 NAUGHTY RICH GIRL 3

Daddy's Bad Girl

I woke up early this morning. I knew it was a big day. No really, it was a huge day! The last few days had been an absolute whirlwind for me. I had met Marcus Wilson who had totally rocked my world in too many ways to even say. He was black though, and my racist rich daddy was not going to like it at all. Daddy was out of town on business in Atlanta but was due back tomorrow maybe the next day if I was lucky. Daddy hired Marcus to work on our house grounds and clan our pool, etc.

We are rich, filthy rich, and daddy thinks this gives him the right to control me and tell me who to date. I am 18 years old and about to embark on my life as a college girl, but daddy still thinks he can tell me what to do.

To the Wire

I had news for daddy. He wasn't going to

tell me what to do anymore. Marcus was the hottest guy I had ever fucked and I didn't plan on stopping. I had given our maid Tillie these days off so Marcus and I could have our run of the mansion. He and I had fucked all over this place, and we had intentions of finishing it off today. Wherever we hadn't banged yet, we were about to! I had spent the remainder of the morning getting all sexy and hot for Marcus. He and I had managed to get the work done on the pool and grounds in the evenings even though we were dead tired after fucking and eating each other off all day.

I saw Marcus' car coming down the road so I rushed to get to my spot where I had planned to be, when he walked into the backyard. I was in perfect position on the diving board when Marcus opened the gate leading into the swimming pool area. When he opened the gate, his jaw hit the concrete. There I was in all my glory. I was butt naked, laying on the diving board, with my blonde curls sexily splayed out behind me. Marcus and I were down to the wire, so to speak, and we had to get some serious fucking in before my controlling dad got back from Atlanta. I was a bit worried about it to be honest. I enjoyed the hell out of Marcus, and I'll be damned if daddy was going to dictate my every move.

As I lay there on the diving board, I made sure to have my hand on my snatch, fingering away as Marcus headed over to where I was. I could tell I was turning him the fuck on by the raging bulge getting bigger in his pants even as he headed my way. I told him he couldn't touch yet, but he simply got to watch for a bit. I lifted my ass and brought out my waterproof vibe. I switched it on high and got to rubbing my cunt lips and clit real furiously. Marcus' eyes about popped out of his damn head.

I did a virtual one-woman show on that diving board. I flipped over and put my hot, tight ass up in the air so he could see my cunt from another angle. I bounced my ass up and down on my waterproof vibe and set my body in motion to the rhythm of the buzz. I was starting to really get turned the fuck on by this point and could hardly contain my juices from exploding all over the diving board. I knew drastic times called for drastic measures so I dove into the pool, making a huge splash that covered Marcus and his horny ass dick.

Of course, I had my handy vibe in tow and I started to toy with my horny pussy underwater. Marcus almost broke his neck trying to peer over the edge at me going to town on my girly bits. I nearly drowned as I gasped, my cunt convulsing around my toy in the clear water of the pool. Masturbating underwater was a whole new sensation. It was like having a refreshed and cool snatch at the same time it raged with fire. The water magnified my swollen cunt until it looked like it could swallow the world...well at least every inch of Marcus' horny throbbing tool. Marcus couldn't take it any longer. He jumped in. Once in the pool, he grabbed me and stabbed his horny tongue down my throat. We kissed feverishly, his fingered dancing on my swollen pussy. I dove underneath the surface and sucked him as long as I could, then emerged back at the top gasping for air. Marcus would playfully push my head back down as if to say, "Get back down there and suck!"

I dove down and then came back up numerous times. I teased the fuck out of Marcus, knowing by the taste of the pre-cum he was dying to shoot off. We played, screwed, and sucked in the water for what seemed like hours. It wasn't hours though, but Marcus did have his first cum of the day right there in my daddy's swimming pool. I was underwater sucking the fuck out of it, when suddenly the balls drew up like 2 huge purple spheres. I released my mouth when I knew Marcus was on the verge of expulsing his cream. I was dying to see what it looked like from the surface. So as soon as he started to cum, I shot to the water's surface. He and I watched as his big black love stick shot the fuck off all in the pool water. It was cool watching the cum as it formed a spiral white and frothy shape in the pool. After Marcus shot his wads everywhere, he nudged me to go lay on my chaise lounge.

I emerged from the pool wet and naked. I laid back on my chaise lounge just waiting for Marcus to come eat the fuck out of my horny cunt. Marcus spread my legs wide open very gently, yet determined in his purpose. I gasped. The magic Marcus Wilson could sure as hell perform with his mouth and tongue. He had a way of treating my pussy like a delicious banquet he was feasting upon. Let's just put it this way: Marcus knew his way around a cunt.

He very teasingly licked my inner thighs.

He'd get right to the edge of my swollen pussy lips and then run his tongue back down my thighs. It felt so damn good I thought my pussy might literally speak and say, "Eat me now!" Truly, this is how good it felt. My lips quivered all on their own as Marcus ran his tongue closer and closer and closer to their pink, throbbing edges.

I really thought I might start to come spontaneously. He teased me to heights I had only dreamed of. He took the very tip end of his hard tongue, flicked the head of my clit a couple of strokes, and then backed off. My body jerked in pulses of white-hot ecstasy. I started to whimper and nearly cry. It felt so damn good having my clit flicked until it stood straight up like a hard mini dick. My clit quivered and stuck out pink and needy. Marcus suddenly thrashed the fuck out of my clit. I wanted to cream all over his black face so bad. I screamed with an animal shriek. My pussy was in absolute delicious agony. I wanted to squirt the fuck everywhere. I felt it building like a fire in my belly. Marcus increased his tongue action, and I nearly came up off of the chaise lounge. I was squirming like crazy trying not to cum too soon, so I could enjoy and savor every drop of his cunnilingus talents. He continued to tease my clit until I thought I'd fucking flip. No one had ever eaten me out as good as Marcus was this afternoon. I was enjoying every moment because I knew the next day my controlling father would be back in the picture. It finally got to the point I couldn't take it anymore, and I shot my pussy off all over Marcus' face. He appeared to be in complete ecstasy, and he savored every drop of my sweet nectar. I could tell he loved the taste of my juices. Of course, I already knew that. I truly liked Marcus and enjoyed the hell out of him. In fact, I couldn't get enough of him. Then I remembered daddy was coming home and my happiness was clouded over. How on earth would I be able to see Marcus with daddy being back? I didn't know, but I needed to figure it out soon.

Daddy Comes Home

The rest of the day Marcus and I finished up the things we needed to do concerning the yard and the pool. I told Marcus we needed to leave a few things undone so when daddy comes home, he might still need Marcus' help around the house. Marcus agreed that this was a great idea. So here and there we left little things undone. This way maybe we could buy Marcus and me some time. I wanted every second with him I could possibly get. He was the kind of guy I had always dreamed of. He was naughty, fun, and sexy, and he ate pussy like nobody's business.

The end of the day came and Marcus had to get home to help his mom out with some things. He gave me a huge, wet kiss at the door and took off down the road. I was hoping he'd return back in time tomorrow before daddy got home. The next morning I awoke with Marcus at the forefront of my mind. I was hoping he'd show up at the door early so we could get one last fuck in. It seems I was going to get my wish. I heard Marcus rolling down the driveway full speed. I rushed out to the driveway area to meet him and threw my arms around his sexy black ass.

"Hey, baby, did you miss me much?" I said and all Marcus did was growl a very soulful yesssss. We ran into the house desperate to get wrapped up into each other's arms. Once the door was shut behind us, Marcus grabbed me and started kissing me with amazing passion. He started on my shoulder and moved up the side of my neck to the back of my neck and over to the other side. He hit on my sweet spot now and again and sent shivers up and down my spine. By this time, my pussy was getting incredibly drenched. My body was aching for his big black love stick to be buried balls deep within my snatch.

Marcus picked me up facing him and held me while he guided his cock deep within my cunt. He held onto my ass, and I wrapped my legs around his waist and clasped my feet together. Then our bodies began rocking to the rhythm of our heated fuck. Marcus started walking and guiding me backwards as he continued to bang me standing up in the front entryway. Each thrust forward I would rub my engorged clit all over his wiry black bush. He backed me up to the stairs and sat my hot ass down on the step at the landing.

I put one leg over one side of the banister and the other leg up on the wall. Marcus helped hold my legs open and then plunged his big black gun deep inside me. It felt so good the tip end grazing my g spot. Each time it pulled against it when he pulled out, I nearly screamed in pleasure. He slowly and painstakingly pulled and pushed his throbbing cock inside and out of me. I could almost see the purple tip end of his angry dick head as it emerged from my pussy canal.

I could see Marcus' cunt hammer dark and glistening with my white cream all frothy along his shaft. My legs began to shake from the pleasure as he rammed me hard against the banister. I could feel my juices running down my leg and knew it wouldn't be but a few more strokes, before my cunt exploded all over his long thick cock.

Suddenly, I heard Marcus grunt and felt his purple bulbous cockhead ram against my sensitive cervix. He spit his hot seed like molten fire against my tender flesh deep inside me. It made me shudder and scream all at the same time, as I wrapped my leg around him and pulled him hard against my creaming cunt. My pussy gushed so hard I heard it hit the wood treads on the stairs with a splash. I thought I was going to fall onto the stairs and drag Marcus with me as my cunt convulsed around Marcus' cock.

"My pussy is fucking sore," I said watching Marcus' cock soften as it lay against the dark flesh of his leg. I could see my white cream ringed around his fuck stick like some vanilla swirled chocolate popsicle. "Go wipe that cock off," I told Marcus as he staggered down the stairs towards the study. "As a matter of fact, why don't you go out and take a dip in the pool and wash all of that cum off you before you get dressed?"

Marcus nodded and bounced off the study door casing on his way to the pool. When I fuck them there's no doubt they've been fucked, I thought to myself, as I sat down on the edge of the stairs and watched Marcus' cum pour out of my spread open cunt lips. I reached up, grabbed the handrail, pulled myself to my feet, and headed for the bathroom to take a shower.

The water felt almost as hot as Marcus' cock had felt inside me. I tipped my head back and let the pulsating stream of water pound my chest making my nipples stiffen regardless of the heat of the water. I reached down with the soapy loofa to wash my pussy and winced a bit when I touched my aching cunt lips. Fuck! He fucked me good, I thought.

Just then, I heard the front door open and the alarm buzzer go off. Fuck! I thought, daddy! I gingerly washed my still dripping pussy quickly and shampooed and rinsed my hair. All I could think of was if he would smell the sex still lingering in the air or catch Marcus in the pool. This wasn't good at all. This is fucking bad!

I could just barely hear daddy make his way into the study over the pounding of my heart as I realized he was headed closer towards Marcus in the pool with every step. And then to my utter horror, I hear the sounds of my screams as Marcus pounded my eager cunt on the stairwell. Fuck! I thought. He must have hidden cameras in this fucking house! What the fuck am I going to do? Quickly I shut off the shower just in time to hear daddy's voice in the study boom out, "Goddamn that fucking lowlife!" "Charlotte, CHARLOTTE! Where the fuck are you, Charlotte?"

All I could do was picture daddy, fuming in the study. I heard the sound of keys jingling in his hand. Oh my God! The gun cabinet. My heart wasn't just pounding now, it was about to come out of my throat. I dried off and slipped back on my dress. Opening the door a crack looked out of the bathroom door just in time to see daddy heading up the stairs where I had just gotten the shit fucked out of me. When I heard him reach the top of the stairs, I slipped out of the bathroom and ran for the study door. I glanced off the corner of the desk on my way to the outside door and knocked the glass bookend off the desk and onto the floor, where it smashed with a sound that seemed louder than a car crash.

I grabbed the door and threw it open. I ran for the pool where Marcus was lying on his back floating with his bent cock lying flat against his taut stomach. "Get the fuck out of the pool, NOW!" I screamed in a muffled voice. "Fucking daddy is home! We've got to get the fuck out of here, NOW! He saw us on camera and he's got a fucking GUN!"

Marcus was a flurry of arms and legs as he made it to the edge of the pool in a couple of quick strokes of his arms. He pulled himself out of the pool hurriedly. He pulled on his pants and shirt and then looked at me. "My shoes!" he hissed looking me straight in the eyes with a fear in his eyes that defied description.

"Fuck your shoes!" I hissed back, "If you or I go back in there someone is going to get shot and it sure as fuck isn't going to be me! Let's get the fuck out of here!" I ran for the edge of the garden where the hedge grew 6 feet tall and ducked behind it. "Get over here!" I said in a hoarse, frantic voice. We ran down along the hedge until we got to the entrance to the garden and its wooden gate that passed beneath the trellis above.

"Did you leave the car keys in the car?" I asked Marcus who kept glancing over his shoulder towards the house, as if he was expecting daddy to come around the corner any minute with the gun blazing. Marcus nodded and grabbed my hand and pulled me towards the garage, all the way at the side of the turnaround. We would have to run across the entire length of the turnaround in full sight of the house, in order to make it to the car sitting in front. Daddy's white Mercedes sat parked beside it, gleaming in the bright white lights from the light poles high overhead.

"Let's go!" I cried as I pulled Marcus out onto the asphalt turnaround. We hadn't even made it halfway across when there came a loud explosion from the upstairs bedroom window. "STOP!" I heard daddy's voice echo across the front yard. "Run Marcus!" I said loudly, no longer worried daddy would discover us. It was more than obvious he was watching us, and I wasn't going to waste my time looking up to the bedroom window to see him.

"Blam...blam..." went the pistol as Marcus and I ran for the car. "Get behind his car!" I screamed, "He won't shoot and risk his car!" I yelled. "Blam..." the gun sounded one last time before we got behind the Mercedes and relative safety. Marcus ripped open the door to our car and jumped inside. I opened the door so hard it threw me off balance and I fell heavily into the car, heard the door crinkle against my hip. I fell into the car and slammed the door behind me.

"Get the fuck out of here!" I yelled at Marcus as he was fumbling with the keys. He finally found the ignition key, crammed it into the slot, and turned it. It was never as glad to hear an engine leap to life as I was right then and there. Marcus pulled the gearshift into reverse and slammed the gas pedal to the floor, making the tires smoke thick gray. The tires caught and the car lurched backwards and swung wildly to the left.

I looked to the front door just in time to see daddy come out the door and level the gun at us one more time. "GET THE FUCK OUT OF HERE NOW! " I screamed in Marcus' ear. The car fishtailed wildly as the powerful engine roared in protest at the amount of gas being shoved down its throat. I looked back over my shoulder to see daddy's arm leveled at us. There was a flash of brilliant flame from the area of his hand. I heard the bullet hit the back of the car with a dull hammering thud. "DRIVE!" I screamed, worried the next one would find its way through the rear window. Marcus wove his way down the driveway with the car careening from side to side.

"You can slow the fuck down now," I said in a more controlled tone. "You don't need to get us killed after we escaped his fucking bullets." Marcus eased off the gas and the car assumed a more measured pace as we turned hard to the right towards the city. Soon we were down the road about a quarter mile.

"Pull in here," I said, seeing a driveway edged by thick trees.

"What?" Marcus asked incredulously.

"Just pull the fuck in here and turn off the lights!" I yelled at him looking over my shoulder.

The light had barely gone off when daddy's white Mercedes screamed past the entrance to the driveway. "Wait a minute and then get us out of here in the other direction! And keep the fucking lights off when you go back out into the road!"

Marcus wheeled the car back out into the road and pounded the gas to the floor again, driving the car in the opposite direction. When he finally turned the lights on, we were a mile away from the house. I sat back against the seat with a huge sigh of relief.

"Boy that was too close for comfort!" I yelled, then Marcus and I both broke into an uproarious laughter. "Yee haa we did it Marcus!" I yelped and reached up and gave Marcus a big high five. Neither of us was even thinking about the consequences of our actions or what we were embarking on. I suddenly let college slip my mind and I guess Marcus let everything slip his mind as well, because I looked over and there he sat with a big 'ol goofy grin on his face.

I looked at him and snickered and said "Marcus, do you realize what the fuck we've done?" Marcus looked at me and shrugged his shoulders.

"Was my black dick that good baby that

you would risk bullets for it?" said Marcus.

I looked at him and rolled my eyes, grabbed his dick through his pants and said, "You'll find out later."

"I can hardly wait Miss, Charlotte!" chimed Marcus. I clobbered Marcus over the head with my purse. Then I considered money. I had about 500 bucks cash in my purse and if I went and cashed in my prepaid cards, I'd have at least another 1000 bucks or so. It was enough to get Marcus and I started on our whirlwind adventure away from daddy's controlling ways and his gun collection.

"So baby where are we headed?" asked Marcus, who seemingly had not one care in the world. "How about straight west towards California?" I answered. "Then California it is, boo!" said Marcus as he flew like lightning down the highway. Neither of us was completely certain how this would turn out, but I did like Marcus a whole heck of a lot. I can even imagine loving the goofy fucker someday. We drove about 5 solid hours, and I saw a row of motels coming up. They looked like seedy motel 6's but they had half ass working neon signs that read vacancy with the V and the Y burn out, but we got the picture.

I looked down at my cunt that was bulging out underneath my skirt and gave it a few finger flicks. Of course, Marcus took notice and grabbed his black gun, gave it a few proud strokes. We gave each other "the look" and I said to Marcus, "Are you thinking what I'm thinking?"

"Fuck yes I am," replied Marcus and he nearly popped a wheelie and burned rubber pulling into the Motel 6. All Marcus and I had on our minds at that moment was the same thing that got us into this mess in the first place. We loved to fuck! And that's exactly what we did all night long and until the next morning. The sun hit us through the Motel 6 window, when Marcus and I looked at each other and said "What the fuck?"

5 THE ADVENTURES OF DEANDRE LEWIS 1

Seduction

I love and respect women. I cannot help myself. It is coursing through my blood stream and it always has ever since I can remember there being women on the earth. They come in so many delicious sizes, styles, and flavors, which reminds me, I better get to work. My name is Deandre Lewis and I am a designer women's shoe salesman by day and a ladies man by night. I am not the best-looking man on earth, but I am by far not the worst looking either. I have my hair closely cut and a bit of a goatee on my chin.

I have almost hazel eyes, which I refer to as amber in color, and all of the girls lose themselves in them. At least that's what they tell me. I keep myself in shape. I try to work out about 3 times a week. I also get exercise by having a lot of sex.

I live in Chicago and I work at a huge mall right in the heart of the windy city. I work at a very upscale shoe store. We sell top name brands like Vuitton, Lauren, Prada, and Gucci. I figured what better place to bathe myself in the presence of beautiful females all day than at a shoe store in a huge mall. Practically every woman on earth loves shoes, and after I tell them how sexy their legs look wearing a pair of my heels, they buy the shoes every time, and many times, it buys me a hot date with them for the evening.

Some of you ladies out there might call me a cad or a "playa," but I much more prefer ladies' man or dream lover. I know how to treat a woman in the bedroom and give her everything her heart, body, and mind desires. I guess the talent just comes naturally to me. I know one thing for sure, I had always had it, and I didn't intend on losing it anytime soon.

I got to work at the usual time that day hoping to make a good commission and to also pick up a lovely lady for my moonlighting job in the evening. I was putting out displays of some beautiful new Prada heels we had come in the day before when much to my pleasure in walks a lovely cocoa mama. She had skin as golden as the beaches of Antigua. She was not too light yet not too dark. She was just what the doctor ordered.

I sauntered over to her and said, "May I help you with anything?" She looked up at me with such an innocent, yet seductive look I nearly creamed my Armani's right then. She was a hot mama and I had to have a taste of her sweet flesh one way or the other. I showed her 5 pairs of different heels and helped her try them on. She truly did look stunning in every pair. I talked her into buying the black pair of Vuitton's, and as I checked her out, I took this time to come on strong to her. I laid it on thick ...my best charm that is. When I flashed my sparkling white smile, no woman in her right mind could resist me.

I gave her one of my business cards and told her if she ever needed a specialty pair of shoes ordered or just a friend to talk to not to hesitate to give me a buzz. She told me her name was Bianca. I told her I was pleased to make her acquaintance and that I hoped she'd call me later on that evening. The day passed rather quickly and I went about my business as usual. I sold 10 pairs of designer shoes and I propositioned even more women.

I got back to my apartment around 6 pm and put me a hungry man dinner in the microwave. I settled down and was cruising the Internet porn sites when my cell phone rang. I said "hello" and I heard a familiar voice on the other end. She said, "Hi Deandre. Remember me, Bianca?" "Of course, I do!" I replied. "What's up lovely lady?" "You still want to get together for that drink we talked about?" she said. "Of course, I do!" I replied. "Okay, why don't you come over to my place in about an hour?" Bianca said. She gave me her address and I went and got all duded up for the big night.

Ladies' Man
I arrived at Bianca's in exactly an hour. I

had my hot new Armani jeans on, with my crotch revealing my massive bulge. I also had on my new Christian Dior black satin shirt that made me look mother fucking hot. I almost wore my new gold chain, but I thought that was a bit tacky, so I opted for a good dousing of obsession cologne.

I knocked lightly on the door, and when Bianca opened the door slightly, I could not believe the stunning image that was right before my amber eyes. Bianca looked like a million bucks! I almost shot off in my new Armani's. By the way, I need to add that I was not wearing any underwear. I never do.

Bianca wasn't either. She had on a red satin lace up corset with her cleavage bulging out of the top like crazy. She had on red fishnet stockings and a G-string and garters. I must also tell you that her pussy was on full display and gorgeous as all get out! She made my black dick hard enough to cut diamonds. I noticed she was also wearing the red pair of 6-inch heels that I had sold her earlier. This totally turned me on.

"You look very sexy and delicious." I said in my ultimate horny tone of voice. "Come on in," she said. I thought to myself, I'll come on in alright. She told me to have a seat anywhere comfortable and asked me if I wanted a cocktail. I said sure and requested my favorite drink, rum and coke. She scurried off to the kitchen and I watched her fine ass as she walked away. I inadvertently squeezed my crotch just watching this hot goddess swinging her tight little ass. She was so fucking hot and about to be so fucking mine in the bedroom. Her body looked like it tasted of one more time, and I was going to make sure she begged for more.

Her ass looked like it was missing my hands as her tits swayed in the candle light...I could tell she hadn't been fucked in a while by the way she touched herself while she thought I wasn't looking. I dropped my lighter on the floor, and when I glanced at her in the kitchen...the first thing I saw was her long black toy lying on the floor beneath the couch dust ruffle...it was thick and black and had a curve...just like me I thought...she's mine...

I was so busy studying the size and shape of her toy that I failed to notice her standing there until I got an eyeful of her high heels. I moved my eyes up her long, golden thighs. I paused a moment at her cunt and noticed the patch of hair above her lips and moved my way up to her stunning face and flashed a broad grin.

I kind of cleared my throat, stood up, and took the rum and coke she was holding out in her perfectly manicured hand. "Thank you, madam," I said in my most charming voice. "Do you care to hear any music?" she asked with a soft, sensual tone. "Sure! I like most any kind of music except country and western." I watched Bianca as she carefully chose a CD for us and watched her sexy body as she lit what seemed to be a black cherry-scented candle. As she put the CD on and lit the candle, I started to daydream about eating her black cherry cunt out. I bet it tasted sweeter than cherries plucked right off of the vine.

Bianca came and sat down beside me and started sipping her white wine. I was watching her mouth move over the rim of the crystal wine glass and could picture her rosy lips all over the head of my now aching dick. I could simply imagine her seductive lips grazing the very top end of my throbbing cock head and watch the rim nearly explode with a raging purplish hue as she tickled it with the tip end of her wet and hot tongue. It turned me on so much I nearly moaned out loud, and I once again groped my head on top of my jeans and I saw her glance down as I did it. Then I saw her take her middle finger and slowly ease it inside her gorgeous snatch. She looked me directly in the eyes as she wiggled her finger in her pussy with a hot and horny look that would make a dead man acquire a wood dick.

Then I heard it. I heard the wetness of her cunt with the furry patch. I almost busted a nut. I have an extreme weakness for pussy sounds. If I hear a cunt that's wet, that's it. That woman is getting fucked and eaten by me and that's all there is to it. Before either of us knew what hit us, Bianca and I were all over each other's bodies. I kissed her from head to toe. I paid special attention to her neck and shoulders. I knew a woman loved to have those areas seductively kissed. Bianca was no exception to the rule. She moaned sweetly as I worked my magic on her gorgeous golden skin.

I slowly and expertly removed every drop of clothing that this goddess had on. She leaned back into my arms, and I picked her up and carried her to the bedroom. I laid her down, then worked my way seductively down her neck to her stomach, and then buried my mouth in her love patch. In fact, I buried my whole face down there and took in the sweet aroma of pussy that I adored so much. I could tell she was relishing every smooth and eloquent move of my hungry tongue and mouth. She was enraptured and writhing her svelt body all over the bed. When I'd tickle her red clit with the end of my drenched tongue, she'd lift her hips off the bed longing for me to eat it harder and then press her cunt into my face as hard as she could. She would then rub my mouth voraciously with every inch of her box as if begging me to eat her until the sun came up.

I took my time lapping up every delicious drop of her creamy cum off of her pink and pulsating lips. She tasted divine like a mixture of sweet honey and ripe peaches. She used her hands to push my head deeper into her love box that was now dripping over with the tastiest juices. I slowly made my way back up to her mouth inching my lips up her tummy and tasting every morsel of her fevered flesh. Her skin tasted so damn good I could feel my cock grow even bigger than it already was. I wanted to put it inside off her now.

I kissed her passionately for a while and rubbed my girth up against her cocoa thighs, and I felt her trying to nudge me deep inside. I finally made my way inside of her inch by delicious inch. She made an amorous moan as I entered her velvet tunnel of tight satisfaction. I kissed her at the same time I fucked her hot cunt and kissed her with the same rhythms as well. It felt like heaven fucking Bianca, and I could tell she shared my emotions on this point. I made a feast of her body for about 3 solid hours bringing her to a delicious climax more times than either of us could count. I came twice myself, and my throbbing cock pulsated for hours afterward. About midnight Bianca kissed me goodbye at the door, and I drove home feeling satisfied that I, Deandre Lewis, had once again taken a beautiful woman to the peak of orgasm and had given her the sex and the respect that every woman deserved in my opinion. I felt satisfied that I had achieved a job well done and probably Bianca was sleeping with a smile across her face right about then.

LaShonda Johnson

After the night before of passionate lovemaking and hard-core fucking, I had a bit of trouble waking up the next day. When I gave my all to a woman body and soul, I was usually worn out the next day or so. I had just gotten to the shoe store, and I was putting up display and sale signs when in walks someone that I was in no mood for whatsoever. It was LaShonda Johnson. Don't get me wrong. I liked LaShonda quite a bit and she gave the best BJ this side of the Mississippi River, but she was also extremely hard to handle and very difficult at times. She also spoke very loudly. That was hard to deal with when you had drank two bottles of wine with a hot woman the night before. I tried to escape to the backroom, but she spotted me. "Damn!" I thought, "Here she comes."

"Deandre Lewis, why the hell haven't you called me in over week!" LaShonda shouted. "Why have you ignored my calls to your cell phone!" she shouted again. I knew I had to take immediate action or LaShonda wouldn't let up, and she'd get even louder and more obstinate. So I walked over to her and smiled my most charming and seductive smile and planted a hot, wet kiss upon her very full purple lips. I must admit that when I kissed her the way she sucked my cock did cross my mind for a split second. I know I am terrible, but I couldn't help it. The girl gave great blowjobs. It's a fact that cannot be denied. As I planted this kiss on Lashonda, I quickly reached back and squeezed her right butt cheek. I knew by the taste of her kiss that LaShonda was once again in the Deandre Lewis fan club and was probably calling herself the president of it as well.

Lashonda spent about 15 minutes looking around at our latest shoe arrivals and questioning me about every little thing I had done in the past few weeks. I watched LaShonda as she browsed the high heels and then quickly remembered why I had hooked up with her in the first place. She was a stunning woman that's for sure. She was about 5'8" tall, and when she wore heels, she was even taller. It gave her a striking appearance that definitely turned heads when she entered a room.

She had deep brown skin and her hair was in a short and chic style that only a few women could pull off. LaShonda wore tight mini-skirts and tight tank tops to show off her ample bosom and her ridiculously long and sultry legs. She was all woman and proud of it. She had style and flair and she commanded attention. She walked toward me with that look in her eye that I had never been able to resist. She licked her lips seductively, knowing that my cock would rise in my slacks instantly. "Hey baby, how about a sooner back at my place in an hour or so?" She whispered in my ear what she had planned for my dick, and I about came on the spot. Then she looked to both sides and gave my cock a nice squeeze. I of course agreed on the sooner in an hour at LaShonda's apartment. How could I resist such a lusty lady? I'd be a damn fool if I did. Sure, I was worn out from Bianca, but I'd find it in me to please the lovely LaShonda today. Yes, I believe I would.

I arrived at her apartment at 12 o'clock on the dot. I rapped lightly on her door and I heard her loud voice holler, "Come in, Deandre." I was sporting a raging boner in my pants, and I couldn't contain it much longer. I opened the door and to my right LaShonda emerged from her bedroom and damn she looked hot as fuck! She was absolutely butt naked except for a pair of black leather go-go come fuck me boots. We'll let me correct that. She was wearing a pair of "thongs." I use the word thong loosely because they were two black strings stuck between her ass cheeks and her gigantic wet pussy lips. I loved the thought of eating her lips off on either and both side of that thin string. I started to lower my head to her bald brown pussy when she said "No way, baby...I am eating that delicious dick of yours first." She pushed me down on her bed and unzipped me. My prick popped out playfully like a spring-loaded toy. She had me as hard as wood and aching to be sucked the fuck off!

She went down on my dirty dark dick like an expert dick licker extraordinaire. She did tongue licks and flips. She teased, tickled, and flicked. She sucked, swallowed, and yanked my balls. She took my whole 8 inches down her big hungry throat and held it there for what seemed like 5 whole minutes. I felt my balls draw up and I swear I was about to shoot off in her greedy mouth when she spit my cock out with a huge force of motion. I almost had blue balls it hurt so much not to get off right then in her mouth. LaShonda was a naughty bad girl who loved teasing when partaking in sex. Then she climbed atop my prick and started to ride it hard and fast. It was a huge turn on to see her huge 38 D tits bouncing wildly within inches of my mouth. I wanted to suck her huge brown nipples off so bad I could taste it. As if she read my mind, she bent down some and smothered my face with her big jugs.

LaShonda definitely put the S in sex if you know what I mean. She drove her hips in semicircular motions that made my cock stand straight up on its end. She knew exactly how to ride a cock to perfection. She straddled my dick even harder now and grinding more profusely than ever. I suddenly felt her pussy lips clench down hard on my swollen member. I knew that she was about to gush all over me, my cock and my lap. I held her ass cheeks tight with my hands, so she didn't try to leap off of my dick too soon. Then it hit her. Lashonda screamed and drenched me down so good my lap felt like someone poured a 5-gallon bucket of juice on top of it. She was one hot mama as well. I was about drained but I told LaShonda to get on her hands and knees so I could bang her hard doggie style before I had to return for an afternoon of selling shoes. I pulled my throbbing dick in and out of her slow and easy at first and then I let out all the stops. I pounded her so hard her ass was probably still jiggling 2 hours later. I bet her pussy was sore for a week! I held her hips hard and tight and let her have it. I came straight up in her snapping pussy and unloaded all that was in my big hairy balls.

I didn't have long before my break was over so I quickly got dressed and French kissed the hot tamale goodbye. She told me to call her the next day. I probably would forget, but you never know, I might call her. All afternoon I thought about what I saw in LaShonda, and what me and her had that kept us fooling around for over a year now. I think that she was under the assumption that we would settle down, but I didn't intend to ever settle down with one woman if I could help it. When we met, she was involved in a terrible marriage and she actually left the jerk. I always felt kind of guilty about it, because I never had any intention of marrying her or even being exclusive with her. She had caught me with a few girls over the past year and hollered at me and threatened me. She was wasting her time and her breath though.

Deandre Lewis always plays the field and always will.

Deandre Meets His Match?

It was about an hour before closing time and I was beat. I couldn't wait to get home to a hot shower and a little R&R. The past several hours had drained me big time. I was just about to think I wasn't going to have another customer that day, when in walk 2 ladies. I had never seen these two before and of course, I was a bit intrigued. It was a black woman and a white chick together. They chatted as though they were best gal pals or something. The black woman seemed really intent on my shoes I had for sale, but the white gal had a whole different attitude. I thought I heard her mumbling over by the Vuitton stilettos. I sized her up from a distance. I felt my dick start to get firm. "Down boy," I whispered to my worn-out prick. But he didn't seem to listen and just kept rising up out of his slumber. I didn't know why either. I thought white chicks were hot and all that, but I usually didn't go for the type that was bitching out my high heel shoes. She obviously didn't know a fine pair of shoes when she saw one. I looked her over some more. She was super-hot to me in a natural and pixyish kind of way. I had never had a girl like her before, and as the moments passed, I was becoming more interested and my dick was turning to petrified wood.

She had flaming red hair a bit past her shoulders that was all over the place and very wild looking. In fact, I found myself daydreaming what her hair would look like in the throes of an orgasm on top of my cock. She had on a white tank top that showed her pointed nipples off perfectly and some khaki shorts that rode up between her pussy lips just right. There was something about this chic that was turning me on big time. She had lovely ivory skin with a trace of makeup and what appeared to be pink glitter lip-gloss. She turned and looked at me, and she had emerald-green eyes that sparkled with a hit of rebellion in them. Then I heard her say to her friend. "Who the fuck can afford these prices for a damn pair of heels? This is ridiculous." That's when I grabbed a business card or two and headed her way. I walked up behind her and said, "Maybe you can with a 50 percent discount on the house. She kind of jumped from being startled.

"Fifty percent discount?" she said kind of in a smart-ass tone. "Yes! 50 percent all just for you, madam. My name is Deandre Lewis. What's your name?" I asked her charmingly. "My name is Chloe." She replied in a sarcastic tone. I told her it was nice to meet her, and I finally convinced her to sit down and let me try a pair of shoes in her. The more I talked with Chloe, the more turned on and interested I became in her. The fact that she presented a challenge for me was an amazing point of intrigue for me. I had always been able to snap my fingers and the women came running. Chloe was different I could easily see. On top of that, her physical beauty drove me wild with hot desire. I was really beginning to get concerned. I didn't recognize myself at all.

Did I have some sort of fever that was causing a delirious fit? Had I finally went over the edge? Had LaShonda Johnson drugged me that day? All I knew is that feelings were coursing through my body unlike any I had ever had. This was all new to me. Chloe was doing something to me no one ever had before, and I had no idea what it was. But I had a feeling I was going to find out very soon.

To be continued...

6 THE ADVENTURES OF DEANDRE LEWIS 2

Hard Choices

My name is Deandre Lewis and I love and adore women. They are my weakness. I find it hard to resist a single one of them. I especially find it hard to resist them if they are endowed with physical beauty and charm. When God made women, He made perfection as far as I'm concerned.

I was not the most handsome man on earth that's for sure, but I also wasn't the worst looking man on earth either. I had my good qualities, and one of my best qualities is that I know how to please women physically and emotionally. I am an average build, and I try to work out weekly so that I stay in shape for my lady friends. I also find that having an active sexual life is one of the best exercises a person can do. It sure beats jogging 10 miles a day! I wear my hair very short or in a style called a high/low. Also at times I kept a small goatee. It all depends on what ladies I am courting at the time as to whether or not I wear a goatee. Many of the ladies say it feels good scratching against their snatches when I go down on them and partake of their oral delights.

I love to perform cunnilingus. I consider myself somewhat of an aficionado when it comes to eating out pussy. I could not get enough of the intoxicating aroma or taste of beautiful cunt. I worked at a designer shoe store in one of Chicago's busiest malls. I sold ladies shoes to be exact. It gave me pleasure to tell them how sexy their new heels were going to make them look and feel, and I was telling the truth. I try to never lie to a lady friend (i.e., unless she catches me with another lady friend and then I have been known to tell a white lie or two).

I have had a few of my ex-girlfriends (and a few in the present) call me a player and a rogue. But truly, I am not. Yes, it may seem that way, but I cannot help that I have an addiction to women. It is in my nature, and simply who I am. I really wanted to look good today so I took extra time getting dressed and shaved. I had a very enticing reason for this. I put on my newest Perry Ellis dress shirt perfectly pressed and a pair of slacks to match the whole ensemble. I also decided to bring out my 24-karat gold chain and bracelet that a married woman I was "seeing" had given me on my birthday a few months ago.

I loved making married women feel wanted and adored. It was another one of my specialties. I failed to mention my trademark feature that seems to grab the attention of most every woman I have ever met or flirted with. As a black man, you would think I would have dark eyes, but I was blessed from my mom's side of the family with amber/golden eyes. They are striking even if I do say so myself, and one glance at a lady with my eyes and she usually melts like butter on a hot croissant.

At this time in my life, I was juggling about 3 ladies in my life, and I must admit it was getting kind of difficult to handle. Trying to keep them at a distance from each other was quite a challenge. One of my current "ladies" was LaShonda Johnson. She was one of the more challenging women I had ever been involved with. I met her when she was married and she got the idea in her head that if she divorced her abusive and unfaithful husband that I would settle down with her, but she was quite mistaken. Deandre Lewis never intends to settle down or get married. I feel like I am doing the right thing because I know there is no way I would stay faithful to just 1 woman. I love all women too much for that. I felt like I was looking like a million bucks when I walked out of my apartment to head to the shoe store. I had a good reason why this was so important to me. I had come across a woman a few days before that sparked my interest more than any woman ever had. She didn't immediately fall all over herself for me and that was definitely a first. She is a white woman and her name is Chloe. She came into the shoe store with a black woman that was a good friend of hers. I couldn't help but notice her. She has a natural beauty that literally lights up a room. She also had a spunky attitude that turned me on or some strange reason. She made it clear that she felt our shoe prices were too high, so I ordered her a specialty pair of shoes and promised her 50 percent off the price. I was excited today because she was supposed to show up at the store today to pick them up. I have full intentions of getting under her skin and charming her pants off, and I refused to take no for an answer.

The Gift

I got to work and started setting up displays and getting the cash register set up. I had a steady flow of customers for a few hours, and I was just about to give up on her showing up when I see her walking in the store. This time she was alone. I nonchalantly walked over to Chloe and said hello and kissed her on her cheek very sweetly. I could have sworn I saw her blush. I led her to a seat where she could try on her shoes. I helped her with them and she looked stunning I must say. She stood up and kind of pranced around in them and looked at her reflection in the mirror. I could tell she loved them. She was nearly giddy. I was watching her and I noticed she had beautiful legs, and her new Prada heels accented them perfectly.

"Thank you, Deandre. These fit perfectly," she said. "My pleasure beautiful lady," I replied. She walked toward the cash register and asked me how much she owed me. Then for some reason unbeknownst to me, I said, "nothing, the shoes are my treat." Her chin dropped to the floor along with mine. She smiled a smile that would light up the darkest night. Then I said to her, "I know one thing you can do if you want to make me smile," I said. "What Deandre?" replied Chloe. "You can do me the honor of having dinner with me tonight. My treat," I said hopefully. At first, I thought she was going to say no, but to my surprise she said okay. I was so happy she agreed. She gave me her address, and I told her I would pick her up around 7 pm.

I was so glad the day was over when I drove home from work. I got home and showered and shaved. I wanted to look extra special this evening. I put on my best looking black button down shirt and my black jeans. I splashed on some Cool Water cologne For Men and made sure everything was just right before I picked up the most beautiful woman I had seen in a long time.

Seducing Chloe

I drove up to Chloe's small house and walked up to the door and knocked. Chloe opened the door and she looked absolutely radiant. She had on a tight little black cocktail dress and of course, the new Prada heels I had bought her. She looked beautiful in black. It brought out the fiery red color of her hair. She looked at me and smiled and surprisingly planted a quick kiss upon my lips. That small kiss made my cock grow about a half an inch.

I opened the door for Chloe and we walked out to my car. I opened the passenger door for her and helped her inside. I got a nice view of her beautiful ivory-skinned legs as I did. She was so sexy I could hardly contain myself. I decided we would go to eat at a nice little Italian restaurant outside of Chicago in the suburbs. From my vast experience with the opposite sex, I knew this was a great place to seduce a lovely lady. As soon as we were seated, we ordered a nice bottle of wine. We had a glass and talked quietly. Chloe had a way about her that drove me to the brink of hot lust and desire. I felt her foot lightly brush against his shim and a deep wanton look come into her eyes as she took a bite of the cucumber in the salad. I smiled at her thinking how great her mouth would feel on my purple-headed cunt pleaser.

I could see her luscious red lips and almost feel them sucking my girth right then and there. I could actually feel my dick getting stiffer under the table and wondering if I should stand up so she could see the incredible effect she had on me. But I decided to stay seated and reach out to touch her hand. She smiled back seductively at me and licked her ruby lips passionately. I almost let out an audible moan I swear. I was burning with wanton desire for Chloe, and by the look in her green eyes, she shared my feelings.

We finished up our meal and headed out to my car. As I drove toward her house, I could practically cut the sexual tension in my car with a knife. I knew at that moment that Chloe Landers wanted me as much as I wanted her. It was apparent by the quick glances and sexy little moans coming from her mouth. Then it suddenly became increasingly clear.

I felt her hand reach over and start to rub my bulging dick through my Perry Ellis slacks. I must admit I was a bit shocked but extremely turned on all at the same time. It became blazingly clear that Chloe was going to swim in the juices of Deandre Lewis very soon. She looked at the wet spot forming at the tip of my cock on my slacks and then up into my eyes. The look in her eyes was definitely saying, "Come on me now!" I intended to do just that and much, much more.

I reached over and slid my hand between her legs that she ever so eagerly parted for me...the first thing I noticed was she wasn't wearing panties...the second thing I noticed was why...they would have been soaked. Her lips felt like velvet wetness...her clit was hard and throbbing as it pressed out from between her long lips. At the touch of my finger, she moaned and reached down to press my hand tightly against her pussy beneath her dress. I could definitely feel that Chloe needed to get fucked and she needed it soon. I knew the ride home would be frantic. I put my fingers to my lips and tasted it. It smelled of spice and fever...and the smell put a bulge in my bone that simply would not go away.

We arrived at Chloe's house finally and I went to the passenger side to open her door. When she stepped out, she planted a deep, wet kiss on my mouth that begged me to come inside and make love to her and fuck her as well. So that is precisely what I did.

The First Time

When we got inside, Chloe took me by the hand and led me to her bedroom. She told me to sit down on the bed and get comfortable. She disappeared to the bathroom attached to her bedroom. While she was away, I took my clothes off and got under her purple satin bedspread butt naked. I was lying there daydreaming about how fucking hot the sex was going to be when I hear Chloe emerge from the bathroom.

I almost fell off the bed when I took one glimpse of her gorgeous form before my eyes. She was wearing a pale pink see-through teddy that showcased all of her feminine beauty in all of the right places. She looked like a decadent piece of pink taffy all clad in her Victoria's Secret lingerie. I had the overwhelming desire to taste every delicious inch of her ivory, hot flesh. Her lips looked like hot wings and damn man I was fucking ravenous, I couldn't wait to dip her luscious lips in my hot sauce.

She walked over to the bed and lay down beside me and rubbed her big tits across my dark chest. I noticed immediately how her milky flesh looked up against my black skin. The contrast looked absolutely delicious. As she rubbed her creamy flesh down my belly, it looked like white chocolate melting into cappuccino. Her creamy white skin looked tender, I was almost afraid to pull on her nipples – she looked so soft. But she insisted...and when I did all I could see was her eyes wide open, and the hunger deep inside, I knew she was headed for my rock hard black dick, and I couldn't wait to see her white face engulf it.

I wrapped my brown fingers in her red hair and felt her ruby lips swirl their way around my cockhead. Her beautiful white mouth was hotter than I first thought it might be. It felt like molten hot lava against my aching black meat. My dick grew fatter and fatter, the base the size of my wrist...and I have huge hands. She held my cock at the base in both hands and squeezed it straight up in the air slowly dragged her pink nipples across the head. I slipped a finger inside her liquid cock hole, and it felt like her entire pussy was on fire...my every thrust with my finger brought a whimper to her lips. She squeezed my finger from deep inside her cunt, and I knew she would be tighter than anything I'd ever had before; I slipped two more fingers in twisted them pulled them slowly out and then suddenly back in deeply. She began to ride my fingers as her entire ass trembled with pure pleasure.

My black fingers began disappearing in her flaming red pussy, and it was so erotic to watch. It was like her cunt was hungry and wanted to eat my fingers to the bone, and the bone is what she was about to get all 8 inches of it and thick as my wrist.

I was dying to get my raging cunt teaser deep inside her ivory-lipped cunt. I could hardly contain the goo that was building deep inside my big ebony gonads. I wanted all of Chloe's red-hot pussy, and I wanted to engulf every liquid drop of her peachy juice. She had the hottest and reddest pussy I had ever laid my amber eyes on. I whispered to her if she wanted me to show her my skills at eating out pussy. Of course, she moaned a sexy yes.

Chloe lay back on the pillow and the moonlight hit the scarlet waves in her hair, and it sparkled like fireflies dancing upon her pillow. She looked eager and she nudged my head down between her creamy white thighs. Before I decided to buy my mouth into her peach, I kissed up and down her inner thighs causing her to tremble and quake upon the bed. I didn't leave one delicious inch of her beautiful flesh unkissed or unlicked. She tasted divine like a blend of honey and vanilla ice cream. This ivory-skinned beauty was a wild woman in bed and delicately seductive yet as raw as an animal.

I must admit I was very cunt hungry this particular night, and I was ravenous licking, sucking, and ravaging her luscious girly bits. I made slurping noises as I lapped at away at every gorgeous fold on Chloe's bald snatch. Her lips were so long, pink, and lush I could nearly make a feast on them alone. I ate so hard and voraciously that she actually whimpered a bit but then arched her snow-white ass up toward my mouth practically smothering me in red-hot cunt. Chloe would let loose a gush of cream but then suck it back in with her red snapper.

She seemed to be bound and determined to tease my taste buds until it drove me up the wall. I ate and ate her pussy but she'd get right to the point of cumming and suddenly stop. It was driving me insane with lust and desire even more so than I already was. She did this almost cum and stop routine until my mouth was damn near numb and I was exhausted. Chloe Landers was a mystery indeed. I had never in my entire womanizing lie ever come across anything like this.

With Blue Balls

The next morning seemed to roll around far too early. I peeled my eyes open and saw that I only had 30 minutes to make it to work. I choked down a cup of coffee and yesterday's donut and headed out the door. The whole drive to work, I thought about my night before with Chloe the redhead. What a mystery she was and it intrigued me so much; it turned me on. I knew if I was going to be able to focus at work, I had to get Chloe off of my mind. I did put her out of my mind for the time being, but I was very confused and I had a massive case of blue balls.

I wanted to shoot my chocolate love stick deep inside her the night before, but there was always another time and another chance. I knew this much. One way or the other, I was going to fuck Chloe's brains out. I went about business at the store for a few hours or until lunchtime. I was starving too. I don't mean just for a hamburger either if you catch my drift. I was getting ready to go out to lunch for a quick bite when I looked up to see Bianca walking in. She had a sack from one of the sandwich shops in the mall in her hands.

"Hey, Deandre. You want to have a sandwich with me?" "Sure," I said. Bianca and I went out to her Mercedes and had delicious Italian sandwiches on wheat rolls. I could tell by the amorous look in Bianca's eyes she was wanting dessert and she was needing some cream filling about a cup's worth. We found a deserted parking lot and Bianca actually got out of the car and leaned against the hood as if to say, "Come, fuck me now!" Being the gentleman I am, of course I obliged. She wanted some of this purple-headed pussy thrasher deep in her furry snatch.

I screwed her from behind in a rhythmic motion that rocked her Mercedes into an erotic slumber. She was taking my swollen prick in its gigantic entirety and she loved it. I could tell by the moans of sheer ecstasy escaping her hot pink lips...both sets. I screwed her every which way but loose until I finally blasted my cock right off deep inside her hungry cunt. It felt good to release the sweet cum from my aching blue balls. I could feel it seep out in 3 or 4 mind-blowing streams.

Bianca squirted her starving cunt all over my throbbing muscle too soaking him in exotic delights. It felt good to have my horny dick bathed in girly bit juice. I would be hard pressed (no pun intended) to get any work done the rest of the day after that cock candy. Bianca was a lunch treat I would love to have time and time again, yet my mind still wandered to the illusive Chloe and all of her beauty and temptation.

Another Try

That night when I got home, I still had a mind that was riddled with Chloe and why I didn't make her cum the night before. That had never happened to Deandre Lewis. I intended to remedy this situation once and for all, so I called Chloe right then and there. One way or the other she was going to cum and she was going to cum good. I mean I was going to make her gush that red snapper all over my face and wet me down completely.

I have always prided myself on a 100 percent success rate with my women, and this one needed to join the pack. I had seen her juice running off my cock and couldn't help but taste it when she wasn't looking, and I knew I could make a lot more...if she would only let me. But that was the problem...how to make her simply let herself go.

I had a few new ideas stirring in my mind, so I decided first to call Miss Chloe up and invite her over to my place for some tunes and a bottle of wine. She answered on the second ring much to my pleasure, and she agreed to come to visit in an hour. I quickly showered and made sure to wash Bianca's pussy scent down my bathtub drain. I had big plans for Chloe tonight if she only knew. The word big reminded me I needed to do a little bit of pre-jacking to ensure my head was as swollen and purple as it could possibly be. My sidekick needed to be in top form. So I pulled out my penis puller, slid the head of my cock in it, and pumped it until I thought my cockhead would pull off...when I took it out, it looked like it was going to burst...and little did Chloe know...I was going to coax every drop of cum out of her she had...and then some...

When I thought that my dick head couldn't get any bigger or more swollen than it was, I heard the doorbell. I zipped up superfast and went to answer it. I was incredibly uncomfortable with my meat stuffed in my pants pressing at the seams to be released. It was aching to get out...or shall I say in?

When I opened the door, I noticed two things. First, I saw that Chloe's nipples looked like thumbs pressed against the inside of her blouse. Second is that her eyes only met mine after staring at the round nut of my cockhead poking hard against my slacks. She looked at me with drooling eyes, and I could swear I could smell her pussy get wet. "Come on in," I said as she slipped past me, the air smelling like lilacs and need. "Don't mind if I do," she said with a smile, "I see you've been thinking about me, huh?" "You have no idea," I said, readjusting the head of my swollen cock against my leg. "But I think it's about time we drop the act and get what both of us have been dreaming about."

"I have no issue with that," she said. "I totally agree with you." We went into my living room and Chloe sat down on the sofa. She was wearing a sheer white sundress that showcased her beautiful figure perfectly. Her nipples looked divine poking through her dress, and I noticed when she sat down, she wasn't wearing any panties. That made my dick bulge even more.

I decided I wasn't going to waste any time getting my darling Chloe to my bedroom. I wanted her body and I wanted it immediately. So I sat down beside her and reached in for a French kiss. She received it with open arms - and lips I might add. She tasted like sweet honeysuckle as we played tongue wars inside a passionate kiss. I asked her if she wanted to retreat to my bedroom and she whispered yes. I could taste her erotic moans within our kiss and then we went to my bed where she unveiled her luscious body to me once more.

I first fucked her sweet cunt from behind in the doggie position being sure to bang my balls up against her ivory ass each thrust and back out. Chloe then flipped her wanton body over and began to ride my black dick furiously. I could feel her depths fill with molten expectation as my wide cock rim dragged across her clasping cunt...her eyes wide with frantic passion; she stared at the man who would be the first to bathe in her womanly delights. I saw her look down to see my knotted thick prick plunging deeper each time she plowed down on top of it. She spread her lips wide with her eyes riveted to my cock. I knew this time would be different. I could see she was beyond retreat, her mouth glistened as her tongue ran across her pouting lips, her moan (like an animal caged within her cheeks) flushed with desire, her throat reddening in the light from the lamp beside the bed, her breasts heaving, and her hips writhing.

Suddenly I felt it. I looked down to her splayed pussy and watched as her flesh began to tremble, her whole body shook and spasmed, and then it happened a huge gushing spray of cunt cream cover my entire lower half. It was as if some dam within her depths burst from the head of my cruel hard cock ripping at its foundation as her cunt exploded a torrent of juice that drenched me with its hot aromatic fever again and again she gushed.

Her cunt soaked my balls and legs with nectar that smelled of raw animal lust and yet the love in her eyes was unmistakable. The power and passion between me and Chloe was something special. I knew it and I felt it. She knew it too I could tell. It was something totally different for me, and I wasn't sure I was ready for it. I wonder if this is what people are talking about when they say they are in love.

To be continued...

7 THE ADVENTURES OF DEANDRE LEWIS 3

Changes

My name is Deandre Lewis. I am a shoe salesman in a designer shoe store in Chicago, in the biggest mall in the city. I also just happen to adore women of all shapes, sizes, and colors. I have loved them ever since I remember knowing they were different than me. Right now in my life, I was juggling three women at the same time, and it was getting rather difficult to do. I had juggled as many as six before, but the three I had now were pretty sharp and good at catching me at things.

I had been seeing LaShonda Johnson, the longest of the three. I met LaShonda when she was still married to a real jerk. She actually divorced the prick not long after she and I started dating. I think LaShonda assumed that she and I were going to settle down and that she had caught me, but I refused to be caught. I never had any intentions of settling down with any woman or getting married. I knew I couldn't remain faithful to her so why would I even try.

LaShonda was a force to be reckoned with but she gave such good head I put up with it. She had a big mouth and plump juicy lips this lent itself to being sucked off good. Of course hot little LaShonda knew how to work her mouth too. I also was sneaking in a chick named Bianca on the side, and hopefully I could continue to hide her from LaShonda. I really didn't have any idea how LaShonda would react, but it wouldn't be a positive experience, I thought. LaShonda had a hot temper.

Then last but certainly not least was my spicy little redhead Chloe Landers. She was a white woman, but she intrigued me beyond belief. I guess it is safe to say that Chloe was my favorite girl for sure. If LaShonda heard me, she'd ring my neck. Chloe just had something extra special about her and very sexy too, I might add. She wasn't a raving beauty, but in my eyes, she was as hot as a woman could get. Also, she had some interesting little habits in the bedroom that turned me the fuck on big time!

Chloe had played kind of hard to get ever since we hooked up. That was a first for me and very mysterious. Also, she loved to hold off on cumming as long as her ivory-skinned hot body would let her. It was a trip to be honest. I had never seen anyone almost cum and then stop themselves. But the very first night me and Chloe hooked up, she held off the entire night and didn't cum. I must admit it gave me a bit of a complex, but I redeemed myself the following night and had her gushing all over her and me.

An Evening With LaShonda

Today, LaShonda was going to drop by after work, and she and I were going to go back to my place for a little fun in the sack. I was a little excited I'll admit. LaShonda was always a ton of fun in the sex department and I needed some fun. All work and no play made Deandre a cranky man. I was doing a few last minute tasks when in walks LaShonda looking hotter than hell. She was dressed to kill. She had on her skintight skinny jeans, a short little top that said, "Don't hate me because I'm sexy," and it was cut off just above her belly button. It was a hot pink color that looked great with Lashonda's dyed golden hair. LaShonda wore her hair in a chic pixie kind of style, and many times she would wear it slicked back just like she had walked right off the runway in Paris. She was 5'7" tall normally, but with her hot pink stilettos today, she was about 5'10. I was 5'10 so it did make it simple for her to lay a wet and horny kiss upon my lips. I felt immediate wood growing in my Armani slacks. I never had to take Viagra and I never intended to have to. The hot ladies in my life kept me virile and that's for sure.

Once we got to my bachelor pad, Lashonda immediately sauntered her tight ass over to my mini bar. "You want your usual baby?" she asked me and I said, "Sure thing boo." My favorite drink was by far a rum and coke with lots of ice. LaShonda always had a 7 and 7. We sat down on my black cushion filled sofa and laid back a bit. I flipped my loafers off and Lashonda removed her pink spiked heels. I knew when she did that she was about to suck the daylights out of my bulging love stick.

I was indeed right because as soon as she gulped the rest of her cocktail down, she was diving on my dick as fast as southern lightning. LaShonda always started her sexual escapades with dick diving, and she wasn't hearing any complaints from me. LaShonda was such a seductress when it came to pleasing my penile needs. She stroked up and down with her hands and licked the sides paying close attention to the rim. As she did her long tongue laps, she made sure to lightly squeeze my big black nuts in rhythm with her laps and strokes.

She might just outdo her usual premium blowjob. This was one of her best jobs ever. I laid back totally enchanted and enthralled by the magic of Lashonda's mouth and tongue. Also, she wriggled out of her skinny jeans revealing her bald golden colored snatch. I swear this chic was on fire today. I always thought she was incredibly seductive, but today she possessed an extra rare amount of ability.

As she continued to work her palatial magic upon my chocolate prick, I toyed with her fat pussy. It was as wet as a peach and probably just as delicious inside. I could not wait to get my mouth all up in her cunt. It looked scrumptious. I rammed 1 then 2 then 3 fingers inside her heated velvet cock tunnel. She hissed a sultry sound that made my cock stand up and salute Lashonda, and it made her spurt a wad of cock spunk. Her cock looked as though it could cum with a simple breath around its swollen smooth rim a taste of liquid delight forever in need.

I began plunging my fingers deeper and deeper still into her red snapper feeling it grasp my hand as I pulled it back out with a gush and some creamy goodness dripping from my wet fingers. LaShonda was getting as juicy as a ripe watermelon dripping and wetting my hands down. I decided it was time to go down on that screaming horny cunt.

I buried my head deep in her lap and savored every tangy drop of her pussy bits and drips. LaShonda tasted like liquid raw sex, and I was eating the fuck out of her in a fevered frenzy. By the sound of her erotic moans, it seemed as if she was enjoying her cunt getting eaten as much as I was enjoying doing it. Then I heard her say in a breathy whisper, "I want to ride your big black muscle boo." Those words were all it took for me to get on my back and allow LaShonda to mount me with her big titties flopping right in my face. I loved watching her swing those tits with big dark nipples while she rode me hard and nasty. LaShonda Johnson was a man's fucking paradise when she very expertly got on your cock and rode it like a black cowgirl. I almost wanted to put a cowgirl hat on top of her head and yell, "Ride 'em baby!"

Then LaShonda let out all the stops. She

then turned around and rode my big member reverse cowgirl style. I loved watching her ass jiggle as she bumped and grinded on my huge pole. She screwed me hard and every which way before she let out a gasp and then screamed her way through her naughty orgasm. Then I felt my pole swell to mass proportions inside of this hot mama. I knew I was just about to blow my jism all through LaShonda's lower half.

Then I suddenly let it go with a low growling moan escaping my mouth and LaShonda flipping her hot body around to kiss my mouth hard and wet. It felt amazing to taste hot ecstasy while you release your dick balls full of hot cum. It felt like my big brown cock unloaded at least 2 cups of penis juice. It was one of the most intense orgasms I had in a long time and it felt awesome. I slept like a baby that night after being ridden like a champion rider by Ms. LaShonda Johnson.

Burning the Candle at Both Ends

I have to admit trying to balance these three hot ladies was becoming quite an undertaking, not to mention it was wearing me the fuck out! I swear the underside and the rim of my purple cunt teaser was so sore I could hardly touch the motherfucker. I was seriously starting to contemplate the idea of spending a quiet evening at home by myself when in walked my sexy little scarlet beauty Chloe. Damn was she ever looking fine! I suddenly felt renewed like maybe I could handle another evening with such a lovely lady.

She walked over to me and looked me right in the eyes with her emerald-green peepers and then laid a French kiss on me that practically put me to my knees. Her kiss tasted like sex combined with passion, and I couldn't resist asking her over to my place for dinner and whatever else came up. Of course, she said yes and after work I showered and got dressed in some nice clothes and put her favorite cologne Drakkar Noir on. The doorbell rang at precisely 7 on the dot. I went to answer and much to my surprise Chloe greeted me with a huge kiss right there in the doorway. In fact, she kind of pushed me into the door and shut the door behind her with her foot. She was very horny I could tell and that made me even hornier.

"Mmmmm hello baby," I said. "What a sexy greeting. You sure know how to light my fire," I said. "How about a drink?" "Okay, I'll take a Tom Collins," said Chloe. I was back in a flash with our cocktails and she and I sat down on my large black L-shaped sofa. We chit chatted a bit about our jobs and the weather. Chloe was an artist and a very good one by the looks of her paintings that she showed me online. In fact, I had ordered a particular painting from her. I was a huge Miles Davis fan and I told her I would pay her $1,000.00 dollars to paint a picture of him off the cover of my favorite album. There were literally tons of things about this woman that totally enthralled me. I wasn't used to these feelings and they totally threw me off guard. I was bound and determined not to let Chloe get any more under my skin than she already had. There was no way I was going to allow myself to fall in love. That's what I was telling myself anyway.

Then I came out of my daydreaming state and looked over at Chloe. My God she's beautiful are the words that flew through my mind when I looked at her. I could feel myself trying to fall for this woman. I looked at her and felt something so different than when I looked Bianca or LaShonda or any other woman I had ever dated or that matter. Everything seemed to be falling into perspective and that scared the fuck out of me! Deandre Lewis never played by the rules or was status quo and I wasn't starting now.

Thank goodness Chloe was in the mood for raw and lustful sex because that's all she was getting, damn it! I wasn't doing any kind of passionate making love moves tonight. Chloe could forget it! I was truly trying to convince myself of this. I don't think I was doing a very good job though. Chloe reached over about that time and squeezed my cock through my jeans. I couldn't believe how fast this hot little redhead could make me start to grow. I swear as soon as she gave it that first squeeze, it grew an inch or more on the spot. We then started to kiss passionately. I could almost smell the scent of lovemaking and sensual sex fill the room we were in. Chloe's erotic love dance had me enchanted in a big way.

Once she and I got started, I couldn't help myself. I wanted to make a feast out of Chloe's sweet flesh and ravage her delicious body. She stood up and dropped the sheer black skirt she was wearing to the floor. I was mesmerized by her beauty and her raw sex appeal. I was also enthralled with her pink cunt that looked so damn horny I could have eaten it with a spoon with a cherry on top.

Then Chloe said something really hot when she looked at me with animal lust in her eyes and said, "I am going to sit down on the bar stool, Deandre, and I want you to come and eat the fuck out of my cunt." I about swallowed my tongue and my dick almost popped off. Chloe calmly walked over to the bar stool and put one leg up on the bar and left the other one dangling. The scent of her pussy filled the air behind her, and I was sniffing the erotic aroma hungrily.

I got down on one knee and began to wallow in all of her pussiatic glory. Pussiatic is a word I made up a long time ago to describe such a moment as I was embarking on right then. I could almost swear her snatch tasted more delicious every time I had the pleasure of having it for my evening meal. I looked up at Chloe with a mouthful of bald cunt and saw that she had her redhead thrown back in sheer ecstasy.

She seemed to be entranced and part of another dimension. I had never seen a woman escape into passion like this before, and it did huge things for my ego not to mention my dick. She was bumping her velvet slit into my face harder with each swirl of my horny tongue. She had a rhythmic motion going that was almost musical as she turned her hips clockwise and then alternated counterclockwise. I kept sucking...her snatch lips spread wide open; her clit achingly hard looking so ripe for a suck...her eyes locked on mine...her mouth looking absolutely edible. Her inner thighs drenched in her own spicy and passionate pussy elixir. She tasted like an exotic blend of cunt cream, vanilla bean, and tropical coconut all rolled up into one scrumptious east or my cunt loving mouth. I lavished her with luscious licks of my lascivious tongue. She didn't just have a cunt...not by any means...her pussy was a flesh sandwich drenched in a honey cream that tasted like an exotic blend of desire and ecstasy all combined into one tasty treat or my palate.

I could not get enough of her tender cunt. It was raging and filled with liquid ecstasy, but she loved to hold off which I had learned the last time we met. She adored being teased, so teased she would be. I tickled the very tip end of her clit with my dark horny tongue until she quivered on the stool. I licked ever so lightly being sure not to flick my tongue too long or she might inadvertently squirt me down good. So I decided to really tease her and lay off her cunt for a few minutes just to drive her fucking nuts. I made her watch me jerk on my big rod until she practically begged me to fuck her or suck her.

I decided it was time to fuck Chloe again, so I told her to lean over the stool and let me pound her from behind. She did as I asked and her pussy looked so eatable bent over like that. It smelled of musky hit sex and the lips were splayed wide open so I could see her horny hole clearly. I slowly one segment at a time inched my muscle deep inside her bald snatch. Her lips looked almost like they were smiling as I looked down at them while I banged the fuck out of her. She looked back at me and also up between her legs so she could see my big black nuts swinging to the fucking rhythm. She loved what she saw and told me to slap her white ass with my black balls. That made me pound and thrust even harder and more ferociously than I had been. I could feel the urges within my ragging body and dick.

My dick felt like hard steel when it power packed her velvet tunnel of divinity. Chloe was the best and sweetest pussy I had ever screwed and I knew it for a fact. She was all I wanted and craved in a woman. She had a petite little body pushing her tight ivory ass into my crotch and begging for every inch of me deep inside her cave. She was begging also for me to plunge harder, deeper, and faster. She said she was about to gush some sweet pussy cream all over my horny as hell member.

She could not get enough of me. She was ravenous for my dick, and it was very apparent she craved it. I think Chloe had the hots for me as much as I desired every inch of her erotic flesh and sexy body. She was the epitome of sex and exuded seduction out of every ivory-skinned pore. I knew I was about to unload a big bunch of jizz deep in her. My balls got so tight I thought they might burst every fucking where.

I felt it when my cunt teaser started to shoot off. It felt like a bolt of lightning shot through the shaft. I could literally feel the veins pulsing and throbbing in her snatch. By this time, she was writhing and bucking like a bronco trying to escape the massive girth of my blazing prick. She was thrusting her sexy ass backward and rubbing her cheeks in my dick bush. She was one nasty little cunt and I loved it. In fact, I was worried about the fact that I was having feelings for Chloe, and I had no idea how to handle that. I felt her clit rubbing on my huge hairy balls as she twisted around full circle on my throbbing wide cock.

I felt the head of my cock almost slip out of her sucking cunt and right before it popped out she clammed her cunt hard on my cock and let out a low animal wail. I almost growled in anticipation of her cumming on my cock... She reached back with her hand and grabbed my nut sacks like she had no intention of ever letting go. The closer I got to cumming, the harder she pulled it as if she was prolonging my cum with everything in her power.

Suddenly, I knew no amount of pulling was going to stop my huge balls from blowing their load deep inside her creamy cunt. She began bucking her hips fast against my cock with hair rubbing her clit like some sandpaper...I could feel my bulbous cockhead touching the inside end of her cunt and knew I was only two strokes from blowing my load.

Then she screamed...not some dainty scream, but almost an animal-like howl that started in her pussy and came out her mouth. Her entire body was shaking...her nipples looked like they could cut glass they were so hard. Her lower lip was still trembling from the strength of her orgasm...it was like nothing she could have ever imagined, but our cum running out of her pussy and down my cock said different. Her cunt gave three little last twitches, and my cockhead was forced out of her pussy with an audible "pop." It was the hottest fuck I ever had or would ever have again. I could smell her pussy cream as she looked down and suddenly dove on my cockhead to suck her spew off the length of my shaft.

She moaned like a sultry cat as she licked and lapped our combined juices from my throbbing, aching prick. It felt so good it fucking hurt, and the waves of erotic passion coursed through me like a hurricane. I wanted to fuck this woman every day for the rest of my life. I had never felt that way before. It surprised me to even think it. But it was possible I was falling in love with Chloe. I knew I couldn't let that happen, but I wasn't sure how to stop it. I didn't even know if I wanted to.

Chloe looked into my eyes and asked me what was wrong. I looked back at her and before I could stop my big mouth, I said, "I am falling in love with you Chloe." I know I heard that come out of my mouth but I was in shock. Did I say that?" Chloe looked at me puzzled but then she smiled a smile that lit up the whole room. She leaned in for a seductive kiss that almost knocked my designer socks off. It tasted of love and lust in a perfectly blended libation. Her tender yet sultry charm was going to bring me to my knees one day, I had a feeling.

I was feeling once again in the mood to bathe Chloe in all of my love and lustful motions. I wanted to take her to my bed with satin sheets and undress her again piece by piece. I longed to wash her body in loving kisses and licks. I took her to my bed and Chloe and I rocked our bodies in rhythmic motion all night long. My cock stayed inside of her for hours and hours. I would release my seed within her and then let it rise to a massive girth and then fuck her and make love to her over and over. Finally, after making love for what seemed like eternity and only in a good way, we melted into each other's arms spent and worn out. This night would be burned in my mind as the single most erotic and seductive night I have ever had. I wasn't sure about what it took to be truly in love, but with Chloe, I was more than willing to try. From the top of her beautiful scarlet redhead to the tips of her toes, she was everything I had ever wanted in a woman and much more. She was the S in sex and the L in love and I couldn't wait to show her all that I had to offer. I wasn't sure how I was going to resist the temptation of other women who crossed my path but I was willing to try with Chloe. She was worth it and so much more.

8 NIGHTSHIFTS 1

Naughty Nurse

I heard the alarm clock and slowly opened my tired eyes and saw that it was almost 11 p.m. I knew I better get up and get ready for the 12-hour night shift at Baltimore General Hospital. Yes, I am a nurse. I am an R.N. Actually, I am the staff and charge nurse for my shift at Baltimore General. My name is Liza Conway and I have been charge nurse for 6 years now. I got out of nursing school and then got my master's degree. I am one month shy of 30 years old. I was dreading the event like the Bubonic plague. I didn't want my 20s to be over with. I still had too many people to fuck!

Yes, I said it. I am a self-proclaimed nymphomaniac and proud to be one. I love to fuck almost as much as I love to suck. The only action that comes before those two is breathing. It wouldn't come before fucking and sucking except for humans have to have oxygen to live! Don't get me wrong I am a very dedicated and very good nurse, but let's just say I enjoy fringe benefits. Fringe benefits to me include such things as boinking Dr. Kyle Buchanan, eating my fellow RN's Amanda Sloan's pussy out in the janitor's closet, and doing the nasty with my patients that I found hot enough to fuck or suck.

I didn't rape or force my patients to have sex with me .They were always ready, willing, and able. It didn't take too much persuasion on my part. I am very hot, if I do say so myself. I have long medium-brown hair, olive skin, and deep brown eyes. My body is my trademark though. I keep it in near perfect condition. I am not trying to sound like I am bragging, but I work hard to keep my hot body. I am 5 feet 4 inches tall and I always wear tight dresses and skirts for my patient's pleasure. My patients are very important to me, and I demanded to look beautiful for them each time I clocked in on the night shift.

Long Nights

I clocked in that particular evening at precisely 12:00 a.m. on the dot. I worked 12-hour shifts and it was killer sometime. I started getting my papers in order, getting meds ready to dispense and giving orders for my other nurses that were on duty. As I looked at the schedule, I also saw that Dr. Buchanan was on duty. "Mmmm," I thought to myself, "I just might get fucked tonight after all." Kyle, as I call him, is hot as he can be and unattached which always makes things way easier. He and I had screwed all over this hospital. Like I said earlier, I am also VERY bisexual, which means I have had the pleasure of eating out at least 3 of the other nurses working tonight's shift. If Kyle wasn't available tonight, I had plans getting sex one way or the other and it might be eating Nurse Amanda out.

Just thinking about it took me back to the night she and I got it on in the nurse's lounge. She had a delicious cunt if I recall...and I do. I was particularly horny that night and my favorite male patient with the 10-inch dick had been released earlier that day. I was so wet I couldn't contain myself. I had already rubbed one almost out twice in the ladies room. I stopped just short of a full-blown orgasm so that my snatch would be so fucking horny I could hardly touch it. I had to stop thinking about that right now and focus on my rounds. I went around visiting my patients making sure they were comfortable. I had about given up on finding a suitable patient to fuck and then I entered room 20. One of the hottest guys I had ever seen in my life was lying in the bed right before my very eyes. I said hello and did my typical blood pressure check, temperature check, and medicine administering. He and I talked a bit while I examined him and I could see underneath his gown resided a very nice cock. He was about 20 years old and very handsome. I found out through talking with him that he had issues with stomachaches and they were performing a series of tests on him to find out the reason. He also told me that he was a college soccer player and a student and was under an extreme amount of pressure and that was probably why he had the stomachaches.

I looked him over well, too well in fact. As I did so, I got even a better look at his amazing cock. I could swear it was getting hard as we talked. I made sure to lean over and let him see my cleavage and hopefully a little bit of nipple if he was lucky. I had worn my Victoria's Secret push-up bra because I knew it showed off my tits just perfectly. As he looked, I noticed he reached under his gown with his left hand and gave his golden-boy dick a few strokes and concentrated his pressure on his ample cock head. He looked incredibly sexy lying there jacking on his dick like that. It made my mouth water and my pussy pulsate and get wet in my red thong. I desperately wanted to go down on this guy's cock and suck it like there was no tomorrow. But I figured I'd wait until I finished my rounds and come back in his room around 3 a.m. That is when things in the hospital were at their quietest.

I went about my business over the course of the next few hours, and I saw the light for room 20 get bright at the nurse's station. I felt my heart jump in my chest. I couldn't wait to arrive in room 20 and seduce my handsome patient.

Seduction in Room 20

I tapped lightly on the door before entering into his room and I about fell down when I looked over at the bed. My patient was lying there with his dick exposed jerking it hard and furious. My jaw about hit the ground but of course I loved it and it got me immediately wet between my snatch lips. I walked toward him slowly unbuttoning my nurse's uniform to reveal my tits. I popped each one out of my bra so he could get an eyeful of boobs. I walked back over and slid a chair under the doorknob just in case one of the other horny nurses got curious.

"Where were we?" I seductively asked and then without warning I ravaged his cock and swallowed him whole, balls deep. He whimpered a low growl and I looked at him and shushed him through my suck. I also shook my head no. I turned and lifted my dress just up above my round tight ass. I was revealing to him my furry cunt. I kept my pussy full grown. I think hair is way sexier than bald when it comes to cunts. I always hated to shave one before surgery, but I made sure they got enjoyment from it too. I wasn't opposed to eating a pussy out while I shaved her bald. If I did happen to eat a female patient's pussy off, I always left the smell of cunt on my face. I always wondered if the male patients smelled it and if it gave them a boner.

Then, my thoughts returned to the hunk I was blowing. He was starting to squirm real good now. I felt it was about time I took it up a notch. I got on top of him without much pressure and straddled him with my face to his dick. I stuck my cunt up in the air and fingered my hole while I sucked him some more. I then jiggled and bounced my cheeks for him to acquire even more of a massive wood dick growing in my mouth. His dick had grown 2 inches easily since I started. I had great olfactory senses and I could smell pussy cream and dick pre-cum in the air. As I fingered my tight cat, it was starting to almost meow. It got massively wet too. I let the words "mmmmm fuck" from my mouth. When I said that, it meant I wanted to cum.

My patient wanted to cum as well; I could tell by his balls. They were big, hairy, and loaded. I felt him slip two fingers inside my furry patch as I slid my expert dick sucking mouth up and down his pole. Damn, he sure had a way with his hungry fingers. As he fucked me with his wet digits, I could smell my pussy waft through the air. I bucked back on his hand grinding my ass and hips harder and harder still. I wanted to cum all over his fingers. He wanted to shoot down my throat even more. Right when I thought he was just seconds away from shooting, I flipped around to face him. Then, without a word spoken, I fucked him wildly and passionately in his hospital bed.

I couldn't hold back any longer and I spewed my wads all over his lap and prick. Then, as he felt my hot cum seeping down his lap, he shot up inside me too. We both cried silent moans and screams as we had a hot orgasm simultaneously. It felt so damn good creaming his dick. I quickly hopped off his spent cock and did the usual blood pressure and temperature check. I then went and got a cloth and cleaned his prick up good as new for him and gave him a quick sexy smile and headed out the door and down the hall.

I got a few steps and ran smack dab into Nurse Amanda. "Hi Liza, is the patient doing okay in room 20?" She winked at me seductively, and then without warning plunged her middle finger under my skirt right inside my snatch. I winced and then smiled back as Amanda took her finger to her mouth and ate my cream off of it. "Mmm, it tastes good Liza. It tastes like you just got fucked." I said nothing but smiled at Amanda. I must admit I was craving her snatch now. "Meet me in the janitor's closet in about an hour." I said to Amanda. It was one of our favorite places to eat each other. "Sure thing nurse!" she said and sauntered off down the hall shaking her ass as hard as she could. I couldn't wait to do her.

Girls Just Want to Have Fun

The hour passed quickly and I saw Amanda headed down the hall towards our favorite pussy-eating hide out. I almost audibly moaned, but I put my hand to my mouth and did a fake little cough so that no one caught it. "Nurse Gretchen?" I said. "Yes Liza" Gretchen replied. "Will you please keep an eye out for my station here?" I asked. "I need to go and assist one of our nursing students with an injection." "Sure thing Liza" she replied. "Thanks dear." I replied and hurried down the hall towards the janitor's domain.

When I opened the door, I saw a very hot scene underway. There was Amanda fucking herself hard and deep with 2 fingers. I couldn't stand not taking part in the activities, so I went over to her and started helping her out with her pussy. I plunged 4 fingers of my own into her and then I grabbed her hand and pushed it into my own snatch. I wanted all five of her fingers in me and I wanted it now. That is exactly what I got and then some. As she twisted her fingers, I plunged down on her hand harder. I fucked her hard like it was going out of style swiveling my hips to take as much of her hand inside as I could. While she worked my cunt over, I sucked her tits hard and nibbled them lightly. I could tell she loved it by the moans escaping from her throat.

Amanda was one hot little slut and I loved fucking and sucking her. I grabbed her long hair from behind and pulled her head into my face and gave her a deep, wet French kiss, and then I looked down at my pulsating cat and looked up at her and said, "Eat it up, now." Amanda licked her gorgeous ruby lips and said, "It would be my pleasure Liza." And then Amanda lowered to her knees and started to wallow in my cunt. It felt so hot the tongue flicks and the tongue plunges deep inside my furry pussy. I was moaning, groaning, and writhing my naughty hips to the rhythm of her flicking tongue. I loved every move of her tongue upon my flower. I then looked at her and told her to lie down on the floor on a towel. Amanda always took bottom and I took top. I got on top of her hot body, and we rubbed our nasty cunts together vigorously.

I sat straight up on top of her hot bimbo body and humped her pussy seven ways to Sunday. We both moaned and nearly screamed it felt so good rubbing one out on each other's snatch. Amanda twisted my nips while I creamed all over her racing strip. I looked down and saw my pussy juice covering her crotch, and then I went down on Amanda and finished her off. I flicked and licked simultaneously until I could she was about to gush everywhere. I was exactly right. She shot her hips up towards me and gushed the fuck out of her fuzzy cat. I lapped like another cat drinking milk. I could taste my cream and her cream blended into pussiatic perfection. I drank of it and then kissed her vehemently and gave her a taste of our nasty libation. We quickly got dressed and one at a time made our way back to the nurse's station. I am sure we left a scent of lesbian pussy down the hall. I hope we did and that someone had to make their way into the nearest bathroom and jerk off just smelling the aroma of cunt in the air.

A Rendezvous with Dr. Buchanan

For the next couple of hours, I went about my duties checking on patients and doing paperwork. I noticed Dr. Kyle Buchanan making his way towards the nurse's station. The sight of him always made me feel warm and fuzzy, I must say. I hoped he'd smell Amanda's cunt all over my face. I also hoped it would turn him the fuck on. Kyle walked up to me and quickly pinched my tight ass. "Hello Liza, how are you?" "Better now that you are here Kyle," I replied. I couldn't believe myself, but I was actually getting horny for Kyle even as we spoke. I knew he wanted me too. We had gotten it on several times in the past, and I looked forward to getting it on again. Kyle walked over to me and whispered in my ear,

"You want to meet me in my office in about 30 minutes?" "Of course," I said while also making a fake purrrrring noise.

Thirty minutes passed quickly and before long I was be-bopping my horny little tush down the hallway towards Kyle's office. I rapped lightly on his door and he peeked out through the crack and I could see he was fucking butt-naked already. I pushed my way in, grabbed him by the dick, and led him to the loveseat. We had made sure to lock his office door behind me, of course. Before we were even able to sit down, he picked me up and held me around the waist and fucked me hard standing. He held me by his strong arms and bounced my throbbing cunt up and down his pussy-lovin' pole. Then, he thrust me up against the wall and I wrapped my long tanned legs around his waist and he plowed me hard and angry. I loved hot, ferocious sex and Kyle knew it.

He wrapped my brunette tresses around his fist and banged me even harder still. As much as I loved being screwed by a hard as steel cream producing cunt pleaser, I must admit I winced in painful pleasure a few times when Kyle thrust super deep. I had been fucked, fingered, and sucked already today so I was a bit sore, but it was painful pleasure indeed. Then, I heard Kyle whisper these words in my ear, "Suck my dick Liza." I was more than willing. So I dropped to my knees with Kyle leaning against the wall and sucked the ever-living fuck out of his cock. I lingered a while sliding my mouth and nimble tongue up and down his stiffened shaft.

He released a sultry almost animal-like groan out of his mouth that turned me on more than I already was. It escaped his mouth in a rumble that was extremely hot and made the whole atmosphere resonate with sexual ambiance. He pushed my brunette head harder down on him and I looked up at him with soulful brown eyes as I nursed his cunt fucker. I saw Kyle start to close his eyes and throw his head back, and I knew he was about to blow his wads deep in my mouth until it slid seductively down my hungry, greedy throat. I had nursed his dick plenty of times before, and I knew all the signs of Kyle's impending orgasm.

I was right in my assumptions because the first little trickle of pre-cum started to escape his cock head's eye. I could taste the delicious jism flooding my mouth with ecstasy. It was sheer delight, and the sweetest cum I had ever tasted. Then, it started to pour out in delicious ribbons of cream. I swallowed every last delicious drop. Kyle always liked me to save one wad upon my tongue and stick my tongue out so that he could see it, so I did. Then, I gave him a huge kiss. I had to get back to my work, so I headed out of Kyle's office and back down to the nurse's station.

Gretchen Gives Out

When I got back there, I noticed Gretchen giving me the eye. I could swear the girl was looking at me like she wanted to throw me down and eat my pussy off. I had to check on a few patients, but when I get back, I would definitely test Gretchen out. I knew precisely what to do to make her come on to me if that was what she was indeed after. I did my med rounds and returned in about 30 minutes to find Gretchen seated at a chair at the huge semi-circular desk at our main station. All was quiet. It was about 5 a.m., and the patients were still resting for the most part.

I got myself a cup of hot coffee and then bent down right beside where Gretchen was sitting. My intention was to get my handbag out and show her a glimpse of my horny and raging pussycat as I bent over, but I got myself one big eyeful of snatch instead. Gretchen was masturbating under the table much to my surprise. She had her dress hiked up just enough to reach her pretty copper-haired pussy. I saw that Gretchen believed in hairy pussy as well. I swear my mouth actually drooled a bit. I loved Amanda's hot kitty, but Gretchen had a big red bush that had me hot and suddenly thirsty as all get out. I hadn't buried my face in a bush in a while. She caught me staring at that copper snatch she was working over with her middle finger. I know I must have had "I want to eat you the fuck out!" plastered all over my wanton face.

Gretchen looked up at me and then nonchalantly dug her finger over her luscious long labia very seductively. It turned me on so badly I almost muff-dived right there. Fuck, she was hot as hell and ready to eat. I looked both ways and then pulled my dress up to reveal my wavy black haired muff to her. She mouthed the words, "Let's eat each other now!" I almost squirted on the floor. I quickly wrote Gretchen a note and put it down in front of her. I told her to meet me in a secluded office that wasn't being occupied by anyone on staff at that time in 10 minutes. She nodded yes. I headed straight there because I had to do a little fingering before she arrived. Yes, I was that horny believe it or not!

I made it to the office, shut the door, removed my dress, and started fingering ferociously. I lifted my left tit and sucked the fuck out of it while I played with my purring cat. I was watching myself in the mirror, which always got me so hot I could hardly take it. Then, I hear her knock lightly. I said quietly to come in. I was sitting on a small sofa and without saying a word Gretchen literally dove onto my cum-covered bush. "Fuck yes." I said as she ate the hell out of me. I think she may be the best pussy eater I had ever met. She fingered herself while she gave me the licking of the century.

She took her expert tongue and drew figure eights around my clit. I visibly saw it pop out from behind its hood and greet her mouth with a kiss. I could feel my clit get pointed and hard. I begged her to tickle the tip with her tongue. Then, she slowly pulled my labia with her mouth in a way that made my toes literally curl. I was humping her face and by this point, I had my legs damn near behind my head. The more she teased my clit and hood, the more my body jerked in reaction. I was so fucking hot; I was writhing all over the couch.

She didn't stop though and she repeatedly took her tongue tip and flicked away my red-hot clit. I raised my ass up high with my clit practically begging for more flicks. I felt my clit getting hotter and redder as she did this. She kept up with the same pressure and motion, refusing to dive in any more. She wanted a clitoral orgasm and that's what she was going to get all over her face. Suddenly, I felt the familiar feeling of a good squirt. I pulled back hard on the upper part of my cunt so she could flick the clit like crazy. I looked at her while she tickled and teased my clitoral boner. She looked up at me with that pussy-eating look on her face, knowing she was going to get drenched. Then, to my surprise, I looked at her fingers working magic on her own clit and hood and saw her gush out a huge squirt. She thrust her hips forward and made her cream shoot 2 feet at least. She stopped eating me for a second so she could concentrate on her own orgasm. That's when I took my tongue and did it for her. I buried my face in her red snapper and ate the fuck out of her. I flicked my tongue on her pointed clit tip. I lapped and flicked away and ate her musky pussy out.

She damn near screamed and thrust her hips forward and sprayed the fuck out of my face. It drenched me all over my fucking face. "Mmmm I want to eat my own pussy so bad. Let me lick it off your face," she said. While she did so, her nasty cunt popped off again all over the rug. That is when I started to shoot my pussy all over Gretchen's face. She moaned and writhed in ecstasy and I did too. We had us a pussy fest right there in that empty office down the hall. Gretchen was certainly a new favorite on my list of most fuckable people in the hospital. She sure knew how to eat the cum out of my snatch and she was a hot squirter as well. After she and I recovered, we got our uniforms back on and headed back to the station. It was only a few hours before our night shift was over. I was sure worn out and I'm not sure if that is because of work or from getting fucked and sucked all night long. It is all in a night's work! That's my motto. I finally got to clock out and head home until the next nightshift rolled around. As I drove away from Baltimore General Hospital, I couldn't help but wonder what the next shift had in store. Maybe we'd get some new patients while I am at home dreaming of getting fucked. I sure hope so.

9 NIGHTSHIFTS 2

Liza Gets Kinky

Hi my name is Liza Conway, and I am an R.N. and charge nurse at Baltimore General Hospital. I have been working there about 6 years now. I am what you might say 29 and holding. I dread turning 30 more than anything in the world. I want to stay young and vital because after all I still have lots of people I want to fuck and suck. You heard me right. I am a nymphomaniac of the grandest kind. I honestly don't think there is enough dick and pussy on this earth to satisfy my sexual needs.

I am about to head out the door to the hospital for another long night shift. I work the night shift 5 days a week and I have done this since I became an R.N. The nighttime lends itself to all kinds of sexual activity. I am a great nurse, but I am not opposed to sucking and fucking my patients if they turn me on enough. I will do men and women. Did I happen to mention I am also bisexual? Well I am! I am turned on equally by men and women. As long as the person is hot as hell, I will more than likely fuck or suck them or both! I regularly fuck a doctor at the hospital by the name of Kyle Buchanan. I love to do him because of his massive dick between his legs. I am also involved in sexual relations with at least 4 nurses I work with, and I never know what patient I will find on my rounds. I am excited to get to work tonight because there is a hot little blonde patient I have my eye on. She is in the hospital for some routine fertility tests, but she has a snatch to die for. I intend on eating her out good tonight if I get a chance.

Nurse on Girl

I arrived at the hospital at 11:59 p.m. on the dot. I clocked in and did my typical duties. I was excited about doing my rounds because of the patient I had my eye on. She turned me on tremendously and I so badly wanted to munch down on her blonde pussy. I finally made it to her room and entered quietly. I saw she was wide-awake and seemed restless. That was always a good sign. That meant that a sexual encounter might just be what the doctor ordered. No pun intended, of course!

I checked her vital signs and fluffed her pillow, and we chatted a bit. I happened to look down and notice that her hand was under her blanket moving in a motion that seemed incredibly familiar to me. If I wasn't mistaken, this woman was masturbating right here in front of me. Damn! That looked hot to me and made me get drenched right there on the spot. I wanted to rip back her blanket and go down on her so much I could hardly contain my moans of wanting and yearning. I decided to see if she wanted what I thought she wanted. So while I pretended to check her towel supply, I put my fingers right up my dress and let her hear the aching wetness underneath. I gave my pussy a plunge or two with my middle finger and then looked up at the sexy blonde lying in her bed. She repeated the behavior inside her blonde fuzzy cat. I knew right then and there that that was my cue to come eat the hell out of that pussy of hers.

I made my way towards her bed, and she removed the blanket that hid her luscious peach. By the looks of it, she had been fingering off for a while now. Her lips were swollen and red as fire. Her clit stood straight up like a small cock. She was flicking furiously by now on her clit and looked like she was dying to be eaten out. I know she was taking hormones that increased her sex drive, and she was probably horny as fuck right about now. I looked down at her pleading snatch and without a word spoken, I ravaged it. It tasted like a warm vanilla cappuccino and was so damn delicious.

She wiggled around in her bed as my tongue tip teased the fuck out of her pointed clit head. I flicked my very best on the tip end knowing that the nerve endings that ran through the clitoris were massive and sensitive as living fuck. She squirmed even more in red-hot pleasure and ecstasy. It was easy to see she was dying to blow her wads all over my mouth. She plunged her fingers in my cunt from behind while I leaned over her bed and partook of her juicy box. Fuck! This sexy woman tasted hot as all get out.

I wiggled back onto her rigid fingers as she tickled and teased me with them. I was so damn horny. I had been off work yesterday. Sure, I had masturbated 3 times, but being the nympho that I was, I could never get too much sex. It wasn't unusual for me to get fucked 5 or 6 times a day. I had to have sex and lots of it. I craved it like a wolf craves meat and bones. I was like a rabid animal when it came to sexual pleasure.

The little sex kitten and I continued our lesbian fun. I kept eating, and she kept bucking up to my face like a sex-starved maniac. I think she might be as horny as I am I thought to myself as I lapped and licked her flower until her pussy petals splayed wide open for me to tickle and suck. They were as pink as a carnation at a flower shop and just as fragrant.

I knew she was just about to cum by her squirming behavior upon the bed. She writhed and roped at her bed sheets and then she let the fountain flow. She started to release the sweet cream within her velvet tunnel. I lapped furiously being sure to drink every last drop of her juicy girly bit nectar.

Then, she told me to stick my pussy up in the air for her to finger off and of course, I did. She did an expert job with 3 fingers and then I begged her to plunge more inside of me. So she stuck all of her nimble fingers deep inside and twisted and turned them expertly driving me to the edge of ecstatic orgasmic delight. My greedy cunt took all of her fingers in welcome manner and I could feel my ample, long lips wrap around her fingers like a vice grip.

I couldn't hold back squirting any longer and I pulsated my pussy and let it go. I sprayed her hand and wrist down until it dripped seductively down her arm. I also drenched her bed sheets. I would definitely need to change them before leaving her room. After I recovered from a very erotic climax, I quietly pulled my uniform skirt down and changed the patient's sheets. I headed out her door and down the hall to my next room.

Medical Instruments

I was in the supply closet a little bit later on getting items to restock when I started thinking back about the times that I had used certain things around the hospital to get myself off. I gathered a few things from the shelf and headed down the hall to an office that I happened to know hadn't been in use and wouldn't for a while. I was in dire need of having another orgasm. I know that sound crazy, but I was. I was a nymphomaniac of the worst (or best) kind depending on how you looked at it.

I entered the room and looked both ways before going inside. I sure didn't want to get caught masturbating in an exam room. That wouldn't be good. I snuck inside the room and took out all of my goodies. I first had a stethoscope. It was one of my all-time favorite instruments indeed. I fingered my snatch seductively first to get it in the mood. I sat on the exam table in a position so I could be sure to see myself in the mirror across from it. I took the stethoscope and crammed it up my twat and then put the end in my ear. I liked hearing the sound of my pulsating pussy inside.

It sounded wet and juicy as I plunged the stethoscope deeper and deeper. It felt so good that I couldn't help jerking my extremely turned on body to the rhythm of my deep plunges inside my hole. I was rocking to the rhythm of my masturbation and getting into the movement immensely. The more I masturbated with the stethoscope, the more turned on I got and I could hear the results of my work through the stethoscope. It was such a fucking turn on, I almost blew my cream instantly. As I worked my cunt with my right hand, I twisted my hard ass nipples with the other.

I started to moan and groan knowing I was just about to squirt all over the fucking stethoscope crammed deep in my cunt. I had to hold back deep screams of pure ecstasy. I couldn't hold back any longer and I came a little bit. I wanted to save some of my squirting cum for the other instruments I had ready to fuck.

I decided it was time to play around with the speculum. It totally got me wet and would probably cause me to release the rest of my stored up juices. I lay back a little bit and inserted the speculum. It felt cold but shocked my snatch into submission. I slowly opened my cunt up and could feel the speculum spreading my horny pussy wide. It felt so damn good I almost didn't make it before shooting the rest of my cream. My pussy felt as if it had an immense cock stretching me into an ecstasy unlike anything I could imagine. I looked down and saw my bulging clit throbbing against the stainless steel metal of my artificial cunt pleaser.

I could feel it tingling as I twisted the speculum deeper into my wet hot cunt. I wanted to hold back my gushing cream but couldn't. It leaked out of my frothing hole like it had swallowed two squirting cocks at once, and from the looks of it, it very well could. I would have to remember that for later: two cocks inside me at once—mmmmm. Two hard throbbing cocks pistoning in and out of my gushing cunt at the same time—as one went in, the other went out—it was like being fucked sideways. There was nothing like being pounded every which way but loose by 2 bulging members at the same horny time.

I started to thrash on the exam table just imagining the naughty thins I was. I was so turned on I doubt I would be able to walk. Nothing turned me on as much as watching a thick hard cock burying itself balls deep inside my swollen cream pit. It was an image I could not get out of my head—or did I even want to. My cunt lips were made to wrap around cock shafts, and the hospital was full of them everywhere I looked. I don't remember seeing a single face at times, but I could describe every crotch in the building—thick fat short ones and long thin ones that laid along their leg like some cruel weapon ready to be discharged. Sometimes, I could see their hard ones actually twitch in their pants. Those were the ones I craved the most. When I came, I could hear the splash on the white tile floor. I looked down to see the puddle beneath me glistening beneath the buzzing hum of the fluorescent lights. When I stood up, the speculum refused to release its inner grip on my still twitching pussy hanging there like some evil metallic instrument of ecstasy. When I pulled it out, my inner walls pulled out with it looking like some greedy baby refusing to let go of a huge milk-filled nipple—the sucking plop when it finally relinquished its grip. I decided it was time to get back to the nurse's station and find that new hot intern I had my eyes on. I figured it was time to break him in and introduce him to nurse Liza.

The Intern

I made my way back to the supply closet first and put away the instruments I had "borrowed." I headed then for the nurse's station and saw Jeff, the new intern, filling out a patient's chart. He looked so damn fuckable it wasn't even funny. I went up beside him and then casually bent over so he could see my wet dripping snatch smiling at him. He looked at me as if I was a rare piece of prime rib and he hadn't eaten in a week. I glanced down and saw the need stretched long and full beneath his crisp white scrubs. He looked at me with wanton desire that made my cunt lips shutter.

I handed him a little note that I had

scribbled down inviting him to meet me in his office in an hour. He scribbled back a resounding yes. I winked at him and sacheted away making sure to swing my tight ass as I did. If that hot little intern only knew what I had in store for him, he'd pop off in his pants right now.

The hour passed by quickly and I couldn't wait to get my hands in Jeff's pants. He looked well hung to say the least. I knocked on the office door, and he told me to come on in. Much to my surprise, he was there wanking his cock leaned against the desk. He looked so fucking hot that I lunged straight for his throbbing muscle and wrapped my mouth around it. It tasted like butter cream icing and fit in my mouth perfectly. It fit like a hand in a glove. I loved the taste of swollen dick. It made my cunts lips expand an inch at least. His cock reeked of too long without satisfaction— the vein dark purple as it pumped blood to his swollen cockhead. I could feel it twitch in my mouth almost as if begging me to suck it dry without a word being spoken. His shaft felt like velvet as it slid along my lips while my tongue tried to encircle the rim of his head to tease out a few more drops of his clear nooky nectar.

I nursed his throbbing muscle for every drop of pre-cum I could coax out of it. It tasted like the nectar of the gods. It was one of the most delicious peters I had ever put between my lips, which made me want to fuck it vehemently. I told him to sit down in the office chair so I could climb atop his pole and fuck him.

He did as I said of course. I climbed on him with my skirt hiked up revealing my hungry cunt lip, ready to snatch his pole deep within. My cunt didn't waste a second and snapped him in real quickly. She was hungry as fuck and it was very apparent. I writhed upon his lap like a cock hungry hooker. I was so damn horny after the speculum incident. I did figure eights on his pal and moaned in sheer pleasure. I honestly don't know if there was enough cock in the world to please my starving twat.

She was a hungry hole that simply could not be filled up enough. I could feel his tight balls lying on my ass cheeks and it felt so erotic I suddenly wanted to wet his fucking lap down. But before I could think another thought in that direction, Jeff told me to get on all fours on the floor. I did as the dick asked. Who was I to argue with a horny as fuck man?

I made my way to the floor and got in doggie-style fucking position. I looked seductively to my left to see if he was about to enter my love tunnel, and he was, much to my delight. Fuck, I got excited right when I knew a shaft was about to go inside my drenched cock-pleaser. The first thrust inside was always breathtaking and such a tantalizing erotic dessert. I looked between my legs and saw his huge bag swaying to the rocking rhythm of our fuck. I felt his rim graze my wanton G-spot, and it made me nearly scream with clitoral anguish. I clenched my teeth and closed my eyes as each thrust was just a little taste of sexual heaven.

Fuck, this dude turned my screaming cunt on! I wished so bad I could feel his huge balls emptying into my hot wet cunt, and yet at the same time I wanted so badly to see his white torrent of man goo shooting all up inside me. I watched his balls slap up against my ass as his thick cock turned my long cunt lips into trembling excitement. God, this man could fuck. I wanted more and more of him. I wanted him to unload his white cream deep inside my throbbing love box. He fucked with a savage demand that had my cunt aching for release. I pumped back against him driving my ass like trying to break his cock off inside me. Each slam was another surrender to my seductive pussy lips.

I looked back and saw his huge nut sack suddenly tighten and knew what to expect: his fingers dug into my hips as a low growl turned animal from his lips. I knew he was just about ready to unleash it all deep inside my horny hole. I reared back and fucked him hard as well slapping my jiggling ass cheeks up against his hairy balls as hard as I fucking could. I was bound and determined that this guy was getting the fucking of his ever-lovin' life right now! And that's exactly what he got as the two of us screamed out in animal, orgasmic lust!

I guarantee this was the best fuck Jeff had ever gotten in his life, and I also had a feeling he and I would be fucking again very soon. I might even fuck the horny dude tomorrow's night shift if he played his cards right.

Another Time with Gretchen

I made my way back to the nurse's station and saw the hot little redhead Gretchen sitting there looking horny as hell. Just a few weeks ago, she and I had partaken of one another in an old office and it was fucking hot. She had a furry copper-colored cunt that tasted like vanilla crème. She was the crème de la crème so to speak. I walked over to her and winked and raised my skirt just high enough so that she could see my just fucked throbbing cunt. "Mmmmm...fuck" is all she managed out of her mouth and then lifted her skirt for me to see her copper bush raging under the desk.

I whispered in her ear, "You want to meet in the same place in about an hour? I'll eat the fuck out of that red bush." She whispered, "Yes." I smiled and popped my ass sexily in her face and went about my rounds. I finally finished my routine rounds and even licked a bit on the cat that I had eaten out earlier just to prepare myself for Gretchen's scarlet cunt. The thought of her crème made me wet as fuck. I went to our meeting place and headed inside and lo and behold, there was Gretchen butt-naked wanking her kitty cat on the sofa.

She looked good enough to eat—so I did. She tasted divine as I suckled her juices down my horny throat. I could swear I tasted prick come as well mixed with her copper-red flavors. Gretchen must have gotten her hairy cunt fucked the night before. The taste of her cunt cream mingled with dick cum was such a damn turn on it had me squirming for Gretchen to eat me at the same time. I suggested we get into the 69 position and eat each other the fuck out, and that's exactly what we did.

I stuck my cunt right in her face and she devoured my hairy brunette pussy hungrily and ferociously. Damn! She sure knew how to eat a horny pussy out, that's for sure. I bucked back towards her mouth enjoying every last lick and lap of her expert cunt eating tongue and mouth. If she kept this up, it wouldn't be long before I gushed all over her face.

She sure knew how to utilize the 69 position for exactly what it was meant for and then some. We ravaged each other right up until we were both about to blow our crème and then Gretchen pulled out a two-headed dong. My eyes got wide and excited. We both mounted a head and started fucking that dong like wild.

We got to fucking that long plastic dick so hard our cunts were slapping together and we were both red-hot! I mean we were red in color and red in turned on quotient. Gretchen was one hot lesbo that I would gladly screw time and time again if she wanted. Each time we would get close on the thrust, Gretchen would yank my left nipple until I thought I'd scream. I would reach for her right nip and try to get a quick bite on that pink pointed nodule. Her titty tasted almost as sweet as her copper muff, but not quite.

We continued banging on that 2-headed dick until it was apparent by our rigid abdomens that were about to shoot off everywhere. Our banging speed increased as we drew closer to a simultaneous orgasm and then we did it. We let our font of cream inside us loose and we both came, and as we were cumming, we slammed our pussies together and held tight in that position until we were drained dry. We French kissed and teased and tickled each other's nipples while we were gushing all over the place. We both giggled because it was a good thing we put a "drop cloth" down or we would have soaked the carpet underneath us. After shooting off, we both had to wait a few minutes before standing up because our bodies were both jerking in post-orgasm trembles. Gretchen was quickly becoming one of my favorite bisexual treats, that's for sure.

We both quickly got dressed and headed back outside the doorway to our nursing duties. We went out one at a time of course. I pinched her ass when she walked past me and said, "Same time next week?" She giggled and nodded a resounding yes again. I simply could hardly wait for m next Gretchen treat. Her redheaded muff was like a decadent dessert with ice cream on top.

It's all in a night's work is my motto as nasty as that sounds. It wasn't long before this night shift ended, and I was off to my house to masturbate more than likely. I know that sounds slutty, but that's the life of a flaming nymphomaniac and I was one in spades! I clocked out and headed to my car. As I reached for my keys, I felt my dolphin vibe in my purse. "Hmmmm," I thought. Maybe I should play with myself on the way home and give the truckers a thrill. And that's exactly what I did. I got to bed that night spent and still turned on. I dreamed about the next night's shift and what sexual escapades it would bring. I could hardly wait!

10 NIGHTSHIFTS 3

Uninhibited

My name is Liza Conway, and I am the head R.N. of the night shift at Baltimore General Hospital. I work hard for my money and I work long 12-hour shifts as well. I will admit even though I take my work very seriously, I am very naughty as well. I am a nymphomaniac, and my sex drive is almost impossible to tame.

I have to have sex at least once a day if not more so that always leads me to having sex at work with other nurses and patients too. I know it sounds kinky, but it is absolutely true. I was particularly horny this night when I clocked in for my 12-hour midnight–to-noon shift. I had only had sex once yesterday, and I was dying to get fucked one way or the other.

I looked forward to my first rounds on my unit so I could see what hot patients were in store for me to flirt with. I wasn't opposed to doing either female or male. I am bisexual and not ashamed of it. I am enticed by either sex equally as much. I went to my station and saw my two favorite nurses Gretchen and Amanda preparing charts. I walked past Amanda and nonchalantly pinched her hot ass and then I walked past Gretchen and pinched her tit. I have had sex with both of them on at least 3 or 4 occasions. I loved eating out Gretchen's red, hairy cunt and Amanda's blonde one. They both also knew how to make my pussy feel amazing. I was wishing I had time to hit the janitor's closet with Amanda right now. That was one of our favorite places to have sex and play around, but that would have to wait until later on.

Taking Care of Patients in More Ways than One

I started doing my rounds and administering a few late-night meds to some of my patients. I was about to give up hope of scoring with any of my patients until I entered Room 5. The room had an older gentleman inside that was very handsome and classy. He was in the hospital for some testing done on his upper back and shoulders. I brought him in some pain meds to help him sleep through the night. He seemed very grateful and smiled at me with a very sexy smile. It melted me like butter and made me weak in the knees. It also got my pussy rather wet at the same time. I loved older men. They turned me on big time. I checked some of his vital signs, and I noticed as I looked down at his lap that he was exposing a massive cock under his blanket.

He only showed me the head just to drive me wild with craving and lust-filled need.

I only purposely made sure he saw me look down at his pink cockhead and I made a slight, whispering moan. This man was driving me crazy. I desperately wanted to go down on his dick. I wonder what he would do if I suddenly lunged my head into his lap? I was about to find out because I couldn't take it anymore. The temptation was far more than I could bear. I desperately desired to taste him in my mouth and savor the hungry ecstasy that was about to ensue. Slowly, I lowered my head down between his legs onto his vessel of passion and lust. I seductively placed my tongue upon the bulbous end of his member and flicked ever so gently yet greedily at the same time. He thrust up gently yet wantonly. I held his dick in my palm and stopped to gaze at it before I went back down on it relishing the sweet and seductive taste of it. He moaned in delightful pleasure as I twirled my tongue all over his shaft. As I nursed his firm cock, he reached under my skirt and tickled my hard clit head. I did a squirming stand and wiggled my ass a bit so he could view it as I feasted on his lap. I could tell he was starting to feel the beginnings of release by the way he grabbed for my brunette locks.

The smell of animal lust began to infiltrate his room like a fragrance dispenser had been pressed. The scent of his pre-cum seemed to radiate from every pore on his cock. His shaft bulged with blue and purple veins forming a road map for my mouth and tongue. I licked each vein causing each one to stand out even more. It looked as if I had put a blood pressure cuff of in his penis the way the veins bulged. I loved feeling the hardened ridges on my tongue. I then focused on his sexy cockhead. He seemed a pinker hue than the rest of his cock. It was enflamed with need. I could actually see his heartbeat throbbing through his head. He could hardly contain his groans of red-hot pleasure. He pushed my head down as hard as he could and thrust his hips and dick up farther as his dick pulled in and out of my hungry mouth like a car driving into a garage. His dick parked there for a while as I suckled deep and then he backed his vessel out again until the very tip was meeting the hard tip of my drenched tongue. I playfully licked and lingered on his cock's eye and searched for the cream like a hummingbird looks for nectar. I tasted the first droplet of whit pre-cum and then I went down like a fiend on his horny muscle. I slammed my mouth hard and swallowed him whole as he unleashed a fountain of juices to fill my mouth and my need. The freedom of sex wasn't just experienced. I ate every drop of it and then some.

Back to the Grind

I went back to my rounds checking on patients and their vital signs and doing some paper work. I felt quite hyper after my little rendezvous with my older gentleman patient. His cock still lingered on my mouth. When I took a deep breath, I swear I could smell the aftermath of his cum in the air. It was amazingly erotic and I almost got horny again just thinking of his tasty cock. I was doing a bit of restocking and noticed that I needed to get some towels from the janitor's closet. I headed towards the hallway where the janitor's closet is. I slowly walked inside and much to my surprise, I saw our janitor jerking on his cock in the far corner of the closet. I wondered if he realized how me and a few of my fellow nurses often fucked and ate each other out in this closet. It was a favorite of mine and Amanda's to go down on each other and suck the other's clit off. We usually snuck in the janitor's office at least once a week to partake in lesbian sexcapades.

Janitor Joe looked up at me and his jaw dropped to the ground. I swear he leapt at least 2 feet in the air. I had a keen sense of smell and I could smell his cock already getting prepared to emit pre-cum out of the eye of his naughty cock. I walked over to him dropped my dress to the floor, got down on my knees, and started eating the ever living fuck out of his horny dick. He had a big long 8 incher at least, and it made me drench my pussy hair completely. He loved how I slid my tongue up and down his shaft so seductively. He groaned and moaned in white-hot pleasure. He was turned the fuck on it was easy to see. I increased my hungry sucks and started to ravage every inch of his throbbing prick by this time. He practically fell to his knees in wanton hot lust. I never let go of my chokehold on his horny meat. I had a suction that would be hard to release on him by this time. I thought that Janitor Joe was going to bust a nut right then, but he suddenly said he wanted to fuck me up my furry cunt hole. I certainly didn't disagree, and I got up on all fours and invited him inside like a horny dog.

He moaned in pleasure when he saw my big pussy staring backwards at him. He could hardly contain himself he wanted inside of me so badly he was panting in hot breaths of air like an animal. The first plunge went deep inside of me taking my breath away. His cock was large and throbbing and pulsing inside of me. I could feel his cock grazing my G-spot with each and every thrust inside of my wet snatch. He felt amazing slipping and sliding in and out of me. I could feel his shaft getting firmer with each in and out and pull and push. I was raring back towards his hairy balls and making him slap them up against my ass. It felt amazing, and I knew he and I were about to explode in hot streams of white cream together.

He started to cum just seconds before I did. I felt one deep thrust, and then he groaned very loudly and simply squeezed and held his dick deep within me while I squeezed his cock with my horny pussy lips. I gripped him just as tightly as I could until he had expelled every drop of dick cream. It felt so hot that I gushed all over him and the floor below me. Like he said, it is a good thing we were in a janitor's closet. Joe's cock was one of the best I had ever fucked in my entire life and I definitely planned on fucking him time and time again.

Liza Loves to Lick

After getting my dress back on and combing

my hair a bit I emerged a few minutes after Joe out of the janitor's closet. I looked both ways before stepping completely out in the hall. I saw a young woman sitting in the chairs outside in the lobby. I walked up to her and asked her if there was anything I could do for her. She said she was just waiting for some test results, and she was a bit nervous. As she was talking, I could see her nipples in her shirt growing hard and stiff. That made my pussy lips pucker in my skirt. I could feel them pulsate a bit as well. I felt like such a nymph, but this chic was getting me hot.

I walked over and sat down beside her and opened and closed my legs to show her my pussy and her lips. She growled a very satisfactory "mmmm" and then opened her legs to reveal her very bald pussy with its huge lips to me. It looked extremely tantalizing, and I could smell it when she opened her lips. It didn't smell bad but rather it smelled divine and made me hungry for it. I couldn't wait to take my first delicious taste of her pussy. I decided I couldn't wait any longer, so she and I went to a doctor's office that I happened to know was off that night and that I had a key to. We opened the door and went inside. We took turns getting undressed for each other and turning each other on even more. I watched her as she slipped out of her jean skirt to reveal her bald pussy to me in all of its glory. It looked incredibly hot. She lay back on a chair and I dove right into her snatch. It tasted like sweet candy and I moved my head back and forth in it very vigorously. She moaned like she was in ecstasy. I could tell she was enjoying it by the way she was humping my face full speed and throttle.

This was a delicious pussy I had happened upon, and I told her how sweet and spicy she tasted. She then asked me to roll over so that she could eat my pussy out and return the favor. I asked if I could sit directly on her face and cum all over her, and she said I could of course. I climbed up over her face and squatted seductively over her. She had an eager look on her face as if she couldn't wait to eat every drop of my cream. I lowered down slowly moaning with every lick that she gave my pussy. It felt so good getting my cunt licked off by a stranger. I found it incredibly erotic and enticing.

While she ate my pussy, I pinched my nipples, which were growing increasingly hard as she licked. I pulled one tit into my mouth and began sucking my own tit off, and it felt incredibly good. I also reached down and fingered her horny snatch while she licked vehemently on mine. She bucked her lower body up towards my hand as if her snatch was telling me to finger it and finger it good!

As she licked, I fingered and we both started to embark upon a hot orgasm at the same time. I started to cum and then I positioned myself back into the squat position so that I could soak her mouth down good with my pussy cream. I screamed out as I shot off, and then she exploded all over 3 of my fingers at the same time. While she squirted, I reached down and bit and licked her tits. That made her buck against my hand even harder and she shot off one more time. I then buried my face into her pussy and lapped up every drop of her delicious cum. I moaned rather loudly as I partook of every single drop. I stood up and we both embraced and kissed with hardly even a word between us. I had to clean my face up and comb the pussy cream out of my hair before returning back to my post.

Liza Gets Around

I made it back to my post just in time to see Gretchen filling out some important paper work in a patient. I walked over to her and asked her if she needed some help. I could see her kind of sniff into the air. I was assuming she could probably smell the cunt all over me. I even heard her moan under her breath. Gretchen is a hot little redheaded nurse that worked the night shift with me most nights. She had a very hot and creamy pussy with a copper-colored landing strip that drove me wild with desire. The more we talked and conversed, the more I had the desire to "play." I remembered then that I had brought a couple of vibes in my purse. I was thinking of all the fun things she and I could do with them. I slipped Gretchen a note letting her know I wanted to have a little grown-up girl fun with her in an hour. She looked at me and nodded yes. I knew she couldn't refuse some lesbian fun.

I did some rounds and administered some meds to patients and then I noticed the clock. It was time to find hot little nurse Gretchen and have some fun in the janitor's closet that I had sucked a cock off in about 3 hours earlier. I got the toys and headed to the closet. I walked in to find Gretchen fucking herself with the end of screwdriver. She was sitting on the edge of a stool and plunging the end of the tool in and out of her hungry snatch. She had her eyes closed and her red head thrown back in absolute nirvana. I walked over to her and handed her a vibrator. I pulled up another stool dropped my dress to the ground and went to town on my furry patch. I loved dual masturbation. There was something so fucking hot about watching each other pleasure yourself.

I was starting to really get into the amazing feeling the vibe was giving my clit. It tickled my clit head sending waves of pleasure throughout my entire body making me quiver. I started to tremble with every stroke of the vibe across my clit head. I looked over to Gretchen who was getting frisky with her vibe too. She kept jerking her body because she would hold the vibe on her clit just long enough to make her body tremble in uncontrollable ecstasy. I stood up and walked over to Gretchen and vibed my pussy while I suckled her pink and puffy nipple. She screamed and moaned while I sucked her nipple and she jacked her pussy hard and vehemently with the vibrator. I told her to stand up and face me so that we could suck each other's nipples and come at the exact same time.

She threw her head back in total ecstasy and started to come loudly and intensely. She almost fell to her knees; the orgasm was so strong and powerful. I dropped to my knees and lapped up every bit of her cream as it gushed from her tight snatch. She trembled and quaked and acted as if she would never quit squirting her redheaded cunt off. I could see drops of cream in her copper landing strip and that was enough to make my bush squirt off. It squirted a few wads of juice and then I decided I wanted to fist fuck myself.

I lay down on the floor and spread my legs wide open. Gretchen started to watch me and then finger herself at the same time. I slowly worked my fist inside my pussy one finger at a time until I was filled completely and loving every minute of it. I could hear the wet noise of my pussy as I fucked myself slowly but erotically. As I did this, Gretchen became incredibly turned on and I could tell she was about ready to explode again all over the place. I couldn't hold back any longer and I knew I was just about to gush my cream everywhere. The intensity of my orgasmic contractions built until I was screaming in mind-blowing pleasure and wetting my fist and wrist down. Gretchen started to cum again about 10 seconds into my orgasm and she came and sat on my face right when she started to cream. It felt so damn good and was so hot I thought I'd never stop splashing my juices all over the place.

Peeping Joe

Gretchen and I finally quit coming and leaned into one another for a hot French kiss. Just about that time, we heard a man clear his throat. We both jumped up thinking we had been caught by the supervisor or someone we didn't want to catch us. Much to our surprise, it wasn't either of those. It was janitor Joe with his big cock, stroking it right in front of the closed door.

I smiled in relief and let out a huge sigh while Gretchen stayed wide-eyed and looking like a deer caught in the headlights. I looked at her, smiled, and said, "It's okay Gretchen. Joe here is a great friend of mine. As a matter of fact, he's a good fucking friend." He laughed and I went over and without warning pounced on his dick that was sticking straight out from his opened zipper. He groaned an animal groan that I was certainly hoping no one outside the doorway could here. "Fuck Liza, that feels amazing." He said as I continued to work his girth in my mouth seductively. I kept sucking him for all it was worth and then I motioned for Gretchen to come over there with her copper-headed cunt. She bounded over like a kid in a candy shop.

Gretchen walked over and let Joe finger her while I sucked him. After I got a bit of a sore jaw, Gretchen took over on his pole and sucked the fuck out of it. He winced at how eager she was at his swollen meat, her teeth raking across the swollen redhead like some hungry animal. She didn't cup his balls; she pulled them, twisting them to make him ease his cock deeper in her throat. Gretchen let him feel her teeth on his shaft as she gulped his throbbing shaft deep into her mouth, his swollen cockhead nestled in the opening of her throat he looked down and saw her fingers flashing through the red hair of her soaking wet cunt. He reached down to pull her swollen nipple.

Suddenly, I put my hand in between them and he looked to see our hands furiously working at each other's crotches. Gretchen felt his cum boiling and knew it was going to flood her throat; he watched us finger fuck each other and heard our juices sloshing in wet suction beneath him. I bet he couldn't believe he was the recipient of such naughty seduction and all-out animal lust. He looked down at Gretchen and me in complete lust and disbelief. He looked as if he was in paradise and then some. I got an absolute rush out of pleasing a man completely. The sight of a man right before he cums gets me high as if I had shot drugs into my veins. Sex was my drug of choice. There was no doubt about it. Joe suddenly spoke up and said, "I want to see you two ladies 69 each other and I'll jerk off all over the two of you." The thought of it totally appealed to Gretchen and I. We did as Joe asked and positioned ourselves in the 69 pose. It felt so naughty doing this for the hospital janitor. This was one of the most exciting sexual thrills I had ever experienced. I had a cunt in my mouth and a cock about to shoot off over my entire body. What more could a girl ask for? I don't think a girl could ask for any more of a thrilling experience than that. I was completely immersed in making Gretchen's soaked cunt come one more time in my mouth. I licked her clit tenderly and then furiously. She ate me with a voracity that would make your toes curl. Then, it became apparent by the muffled moans and the smell of sex in the room that all three of us were going to have a 3-way orgasm. Joe started it and closed his eyes and let a long groan escape his mouth as he started showering Gretchen and me with hot dick cum.

Then, Gretchen and I started to have our mutual orgasms. I could feel my entire body grow warm from the top of my head to the tips of my curled toes. As the heat flooded me, I knew this was going to be an intense orgasm that I wouldn't soon forget. I could tell by her squirming body and the way she straightened out her legs in a rigid way that Gretchen was also about to cum. We both then came at once. The moans that were muffled by pussy were loud and sexy. This made Joe shoot another wad all over us. It seemed as if this orgasmic ride would last for hours. I felt my whole body literally cum. I trembled and Gretchen jerked as she squirted her final cream deep into my mouth. We were a trio of molten cum and hot lust. After our unexpected but perfect threesome, we walked out of the janitor's closet spent and satisfied. Joe said, "See ya later, ladies. Same time tomorrow night?" He winked at us as Gretchen and I giggled and made our way back to the nurse's station. I wondered if anyone ever knew that Gretchen and I had just had the best oral sex in the world. I laughed to myself and made my way down the hall to a new patient's room. I wondered what he would be like. I adjusted my cleavage and made my way inside and smiled and said, "Hi, I'm Liza. I'll be your R.N. tonight. I will make you extremely comfortable, and if you need anything just let me know."

AUTHOR'S NOTE

Readers: I want to expand a few of the stories to see where the characters can be explored further. If there are any of the stories that you would like to read more about again, I'd love to hear from you!

Visit my blog at www.tenaseldan.com

Join my newsletter for free exclusive previews www.tenaseldan.com/in

Follow me on Twitter at www.twitter.com/tenaseldan

Like my page on Facebook at www.facebook.com/tenaseldan

Discover my books at major ebook retailers everywhere.